Books by Shirleen Davies

Historical Western Romance Series

MacLarens of Fire Mountain

Tougher than the Rest, Book One
Faster than the Rest, Book Two
Harder than the Rest, Book Three
Stronger than the Rest, Book Four
Deadlier than the Rest, Book Five
Wilder than the Rest, Book Six

Redemption Mountain

Redemption's Edge, Book One
Wildfire Creek, Book Two
Sunrise Ridge, Book Three
Dixie Moon, Book Four
Survivor Pass, Book Five
Promise Trail, Book Six
Deep River, Book Seven
Courage Canyon, Book Eight
Forsaken Falls, Book Nine, Coming next in the series!

MacLarens of Boundary Mountain

Colin's Quest, Book One,
Brodie's Gamble, Book Two
Quinn's Honor, Book Three
Sam's Legacy, Book Four
Heather's Choice, Book Five
Nate's Destiny, Book Six, Coming next in the series!

<u>***Contemporary Romance Series***</u>

MacLarens of Fire Mountain

Second Summer, Book One
Hard Landing, Book Two
One More Day, Book Three
All Your Nights, Book Four
Always Love You, Book Five
Hearts Don't Lie, Book Six
No Getting Over You, Book Seven
'Til the Sun Comes Up, Book Eight
Foolish Heart, Book Nine
Forever Love, Book Ten, Coming next in the series!

Peregrine Bay

Reclaiming Love, Book One, A Novella
Our Kind of Love, Book Two

Burnt River

Shane's Burden, Book One by Peggy Henderson
Thorn's Journey, Book Two by Shirleen Davies
Aqua's Achilles, Book Three by Kate Cambridge
Ashley's Hope, Book Four by Amelia Adams
Harpur's Secret, Book Five by Kay P. Dawson
Mason's Rescue, Book Six by Peggy L. Henderson
Del's Choice, Book Seven by Shirleen Davies
Ivy's Search, Book Eight by Kate Cambridge
Phoebe's Fate, Book Nine by Amelia Adams
Brody's Shelter, Book Ten by Kay P. Dawson
Boone's Surrender, Book Eleven by Shirleen Davies
Watch for more books in the series!

The best way to stay in touch is to subscribe to my newsletter. Go to *www.shirleendavies.com* and subscribe in the box at the top of the right column that asks for your email. You'll be notified of new books before they are released, have chances to win great prizes, and receive other subscriber-only specials.

Boone's Surrender

Burnt River Contemporary Western Romance Series

SHIRLEEN DAVIES

Book Eleven in the Burnt River Contemporary Western Romance Series

I care about quality, so if you find something in error, please contact me via email at
shirleen@shirleendavies.com

Description

Welcome to **Burnt River,** a new series of Contemporary Western Romance stories set in the fictional town of Burnt River, Montana. Brought to you by Shirleen Davies, Peggy L .Henderson, Kay P. Dawson, Amelia Adams, and Kate Cambridge.

Boone's Surrender, Book Eleven, Burnt River Contemporary Western Romance Series, by Shirleen Davies.

Daniel "Boone" Macklin has a lot to learn. Going from a bachelor rancher to the father of a six-year-old boy hadn't been in his plans. Like almost everything else in his life, he doesn't hesitate to face his new responsibilities head-on. The one regret he has is not facing the truth about his feelings for the woman he still loves.

Willow Robinson is determined to put the tragedy from her past behind her—as well as her love for the youngest Macklin brother. Forgiveness she can offer. Forgetting is something she'd been unable to achieve.

It's been three years since the heartbreaking night that changed their lives. In Boone's mind, continuing to act as if Willow and their close friendship since childhood is over no longer makes sense. Convincing her they deserve a second chance presents more of a challenge than training the green broke horses on his ranch.

As their tenuous connection begins to rebuild, a danger to their families threatens to destroy whatever future they may still have.

Every step toward a future, every memory of the past presents obstacles neither may be able to overcome. Can their wounded hearts allow them to deal with the present crisis, or will it sever any chance of rebuilding the love neither wants to admit?

Boone's Surrender, book eleven in the Burnt River Contemporary Western Romance Series, is a stand-alone, full-length novel with an HEA and no cliffhanger.

Burnt River Contemporary Western Romance books:

Book 1 – Shane's Burden by Peggy L. Henderson
Book 2 – Thorn's Journey by Shirleen Davies
Book 3 – Aqua's Achilles by Kate Cambridge
Book 4 – Ashley's Hope by Amelia Adams
Book 5 – Harpur's Secret by Kay P. Dawson
Book 6 – Mason's Rescue by Peggy L. Henderson
Book 7 – Del's Choice by Shirleen Davies
Book 8 – Ivy's Search by Kate Cambridge
Book 9 – Phoebe's Fate by Amelia Adams
Book 10 – Brody's Shelter by Kay P. Dawson
Book 11 – Boone's Surrender by Shirleen Davies

Visit my website for a list of characters for each series.

http://www.shirleendavies.com/character-list.html

Acknowledgements

Many thanks to my husband, Richard, for always being by my side during this wonderful adventure. Your support, insights, and suggestions are greatly appreciated.

As always, many thanks to my editor, Kim Young, proofreader, Alicia Carmical, Joseph Murray, who is superb at formatting my books for print and electronic versions, my cover designer, Collin Henderson.

Boone's Surrender

Prologue

Burnt River, Montana

Daniel "Boone" Macklin looked into the distance, thinking this should have been the same as any other day. He should be checking his few head of cattle and the horses the Macklins bred and trained for clients throughout the western United States. He should be anywhere but here, holding five-year-old Tyler's hand at the memorial service for his mother.

The clear, warm morning would've had many people preparing for a beautiful weekend, not standing in small groups at the graveside service for a young woman who died too soon. It reminded him of another memorial service he'd attended months before. Many of the same people honoring Jenny Davis today also paid their respects to Mike Weiker, a well-respected and beloved high school teacher who'd also died much too early.

Tyler's hand clutched Boone's. Feeling the boy's body tremble, he leaned down, scooping him into his arms. As the minister spoke the final prayer, Boone's gaze wandered over the crowd.

Jenny talked of friends, people she cared about in Burnt River, and they all came out to honor her life today. His back stiffened when he saw Willow Robinson across from him, standing with her parents. He'd never heard Jenny speak of Willow, had no idea they'd been friends, or at least close enough the Robinsons wanted to pay their respects.

Willow's eyes met his for a brief moment before she shifted them toward Jenny's coffin, then lowered her gaze. For an instant, Boone saw an intense look of despair on her face, mirroring his own misery. He'd made so many mistakes in his life, Willow being the biggest. If only—

"We'll drive you back to the ranch." The voice of his oldest brother, Thorn, shook him out of the depressing path his thoughts had taken.

Nodding, he set Tyler on the ground, grabbing his hand. A few minutes later, they'd said their last goodbyes to Jenny and turned toward Thorn's truck. Glancing up, he once again saw Willow looking at him, her soft blue eyes focused on him and Tyler for several seconds before she turned away to join her parents. This time, he recognized the look of regret on her face.

A wave of intense pain gripped his chest as she moved away, not once looking back.

Thorn's wife, Grace, placed a hand on Boone's arm. "We should probably leave. The house will be full of guests soon."

Pushing aside thoughts of Willow, he forced himself to concentrate on getting through today. There'd be plenty of time to dwell on the mistakes of his past and the future he'd let slip through his fingers.

Jenny's death triggered several events, the biggest one involving the young boy beside him. A few months ago, the ranch, his horses, and having a good time on Saturday nights were his biggest concerns.

Although they'd never dated, never been a couple, he and Jenny had formed a strong friendship. She had no family and never married Tyler's father. When they knew her time was short, Boone had hesitated only a moment when she asked if he'd consider adopting Tyler upon her death.

As they drove away from the cemetery, the responsibility Boone accepted began to feel real, settling in his bones, bringing with it a cold chill of panic. Not for the first time, he wondered what he'd been thinking in believing he could be a role model. How in the world could he raise a young boy when he sometimes still felt like a kid himself?

Chapter One

A few months later...

"Daddy, wake up."

Daddy. Boone tried to make sense of the name he heard in the distance as he snuggled into his covers. Feeling a small hand on his cheek, he flinched as tiny fingers worked to open an eyelid.

"Daddy...get up."

His eyes opened to slits, reality slapping him in the face. A few months ago, Tyler was five years old and called him Uncle Boone. After turning six and the adoption becoming final, he started calling him daddy. Boone still couldn't quite wrap his brain around it.

"What is it, buddy?" His voice sounded as if he'd swallowed a mouthful of sand.

"It's Uncle Thorn and Uncle Del. They're waiting for you in the barn."

Boone sat straight up in bed. The barn, his brothers, Saturday morning...his fogged brain began to clear. Tyler tugged on his hand.

"Come on, Daddy. Uncle Thorn said he'd throw a bucket of water on you if you weren't down in five minutes." Giggling, he dropped Boone's hand and ran to the door. "I'll go tell them you're awake. Okay?"

Scrubbing both hands down his face, he nodded, knowing he'd be in for a full day of ribbing from his brothers. He was usually the one standing outside, checking his watch and tapping his boot on the ground, waiting for them to arrive. Ever since Tyler came into his life, he'd never quite regained his rhythm.

Twice each month, his brothers gave up their Saturdays to help on the family ranch. Del, the sheriff in Burnt River, and Thorn, the owner of Scorpion Custom Motorcycles, knew as much about ranching as he did. Unlike him, their passion didn't consist of breeding and training quality horses or running a few head of cattle. Boone couldn't imagine doing anything else.

Stretching his arms above his head, he yawned, working the kinks out of his neck. His brain told him to get moving, while his body begged him to lay back down. As always, he listened to his brain.

Standing, he made quick work of dressing, grabbing his boots before taking the steps downstairs. The smell of brewing coffee hit him the instant he hit the bottom step. Laughter followed a second later. Del and Thorn sat at the kitchen table, holding giant cups filled to the brim. Tyler sat between them, a glass of orange juice in front of him and a big smile on his face. Boone dropped his boots next to the table and walked to the counter.

"Geez, man. You look like..." Thorn's voice trailed off when Tyler started to giggle. "Well, something like the mice the barn cats used to drag onto the porch."

"We have a cat."

Thorn ruffled the hair on the boy's head. "I know, Ty. It's always a good idea to have a few mousers on the ranch."

Boone listened to the conversation as he poured himself coffee, adding a couple teaspoons of sugar. He didn't know how he would've made it through these last few months without the help of his brothers and their wives. Thorn's wife, Grace, in addition to being one of the best horse trainers in the state, was studying to be a teacher. Del's wife, Amy, worked at Gray Wolf Outfitters, a company founded by Grace's father. Both loved children, as did their husbands. Without the support of his family, Boone would've been lost.

Del rested his arms on the table, glancing over at Boone. "Looks like you're low on a few supplies, brother."

Taking a sip of coffee, Boone nodded. "I got a call yesterday. They're ready to be picked up at Robinson's. I just didn't have time after picking up Ty. I forgot they close a little early on Fridays."

Thorn rinsed his cup and set it next to the sink. "Do you want to head in now? Del and I will keep Ty busy in the barn while you're gone."

Del saw the way Boone's shoulders tensed at the thought of going into Robinson's Feed and Tack on a Saturday morning. Without a doubt, he'd run into Willow, an encounter guaranteed to ruin his brother's weekend. They had a history, one Boone had shared with Del but hadn't yet confided in Thorn.

"I'll go." Del rinsed his own cup. "There are some things I need to pick up myself." He saw the instant his brother relaxed.

Walking to a bulletin board next to the old wall phone, Boone unpinned the list, handing it to Del. "Thanks, man." Grabbing keys from a hook, he tossed them to Del. "Take my truck. It's gassed up and the back is empty."

"Bear claws," Thorn said as Del started for the front door.

Glancing over his shoulder, Del's brows furrowed. "What about bear claws?"

"The bakery is next door to Robinson's." Thorn reached into his pocket, holding out a twenty. "Grab some food while you're there."

Chuckling, Del waved his hand. "Save your money. I've got this."

Stuffing the money back into his pocket, Thorn smiled. "He takes the bait every time."

Boone filled his cup once more, adding sugar, then sat down at the table. "Don't think Del doesn't know what you're up to. He's keeping a tab, and one day, he'll ask to collect." Reaching down, he pulled on his boots, then sat back.

"Hell, he doesn't need a tab to ask favors of me. And neither do you." Thorn looked at Tyler. "You ready to put in a full day of man's work, Ty?"

"Do I get a bear claw?"

Shaking his head, Thorn walked to the door. "The bargaining sure does start young."

Willow Robinson waved to the elderly rancher and his wife as they climbed into their old Chevy truck for the ride home. They'd been coming to Robinson's Feed and Tack for their supplies since she was a girl, when her father brought her in on Saturdays, the same as his father had done.

Through good times and bad, the couple always had smiles on their faces and a kind word for her. Even today, they'd patted her shoulder, as if she were a girl of twelve instead of a mature woman of twenty-seven, and invited her to their sixtieth wedding anniversary. All five of their children would be there, along with fifteen grandchildren.

She let out a slow breath, resting a hand on her stomach, watching as they drove away. As a child, she'd wanted nothing more than to find love, marry, and have children, living a life like her parents, grandparents, and the couple who'd be celebrating their sixtieth anniversary. It had taken a tragic accident for her to accept the man her heart wanted didn't feel the same.

Shaking her head at the silly girlish dream, Willow walked back inside, stopping at the sight of Del Macklin coming in the front door.

"Hey, Willow." He waved, a smile on his handsome face. "I need to pick up the supplies for the ranch."

"Good morning, Sheriff." She looked behind him, hoping he'd come alone. She didn't want to start her weekend with a bitter taste in her mouth.

"It's still Del. Sheriff is for when I'm wearing my uniform and sporting handcuffs." He followed her gaze. "Uh, Boone isn't with me."

She startled, straightening at his comment, her chin lifting a fraction. "I don't give two wits about your brother, Del. I'm just surprised you came alone, given how much is on the order."

Studying her face, Del saw the strain, understood why she had no desire to see Boone. It saddened him his brother had managed to lose a gem such as Willow.

"Let's see." She scanned the orders, pulling up the one for the Macklin ranch. "I think we have it all ready for you out back. Come with me and we'll check it out."

"You're not here alone today, are you?"

"Two men are out sick. At least that's what their phone messages said. The new man I hired last week got a better offer in Missoula. Thank goodness for Harry."

"He's been working for you since, well...I can't remember when I first saw him."

Willow chuckled. "That's because you were in diapers when Harry started working here. It's his day off, but when I called, he came right in. I don't know what I'd do without him. Here we are." She pointed to a large pile of goods near the double doors in back. "If you want to pull the truck back here, I'll help you load up. It shouldn't take us any time at all."

Fifteen minutes later, Del signed for the supplies.

"You should come for dinner at our place, Willow. Amy would love to have some company. Or, better yet, let's meet for dinner at Doc's. That way no one has to cook."

"Sounds good. Let me know what works for you and I'll be there."

"How about Tuesday? I work an early shift and Amy gets off by five."

Willow nodded. "Perfect."

"You don't want to check your calendar?" From what Del heard, she had no shortage of men asking her out. Although he'd also heard she never accepted.

"Nope. Tuesday is great, and I love Doc's. I understand he came up with another new dish he's encouraging everyone to try."

Diego "Doc" Martinez owned Doc's Grill and Tavern. An ex-army medic, he'd gotten as far away from doctoring as possible when he got out of the service. He loved coming up with new recipes and providing samples to anyone willing to be a personal taster.

"Willow, Doc is always coming up with a new dish. See you Tuesday." Tipping his hat, Del drove off. For an instant, he considered inviting Boone, then thought better of it. He valued his life too much to even suggest it.

"I've got to find me a new farrier." Boone finished shoeing the big gelding, dropping the hoof and stepping away.

"What happened to Old Tom?" Thorn laid the pitchfork aside, swiping an arm across his forehead.

"He got old. Left to be with his daughter in Kansas. Or was it Missouri." Boone's mouth twisted as he thought about it. "Anyway, he's gone. I'm thinking of one of those traveling farriers. Shane Taggert uses one sometimes and is real happy with him."

"How's Shane doing anyway? I don't see him in town much."

"That's because you always have your head buried in a motorcycle engine, Thorn. You need to get out more. As far as I know, Shane and Alley are doing fine. I'm still amazed at Mason's recovery. Who would've thought he'd walk again and continue practicing after his accident."

Thorn nodded. "A lot of that has to do with Lori and her support."

Boone thought about the different couples who'd come together in Burnt River as a result of attending Mike Weiker's memorial service. Besides his own brothers and the Taggerts, there were Aqua and Blake, Harpur and Sam, Ashley and Josh, and so many others. His life had also changed in a way he'd never imagined.

"Daddy, look what I found!" Tyler came running up to him, holding out a wriggling brownish-gray lizard, its mouth open, tiny, sharp teeth showing its displeasure.

Kneeling down, Boone's eyes widened at the writhing reptile. "That's one of the biggest lizards I've ever seen, Ty. Where'd you find him?"

"Over there." He dropped one hand to point behind him, almost losing his catch in the process. "Can I keep him, Daddy?" Tyler jumped up and down, his eyes full of hope.

Boone looked up at Thorn, who leaned against a post, enjoying the exchange but offering no help.

"Lizards aren't meant to be caged up, son."

"Please, Daddy." Tyler's lower lip jutted out, a cute response that didn't sway Boone...much.

"Tell you what. We'll keep him overnight, then set him free tomorrow."

Scrunching his face, Tyler thought about it for a bit before nodding. "Okay." Turning, he ran toward the house, the door banging closed behind him.

"And he's going to be keeping the lizard in what?" Thorn asked, not hiding the smirk on his face.

Standing, Boone walked back to the horse he'd been tending. "Same as us. A shoebox. It's just for one night. What could possibly happen?"

Thorn opened his mouth to answer, then shot a glance over his shoulder at the sound of a truck. "Looks like Del's back. Time to get some real work done around here."

"Let's unload the truck, then I'll go get Ty. He'll need to ride out with us."

Tyler bounced alongside Boone as they checked on the dozen head of cattle on the ranch. Unlike the horses, which he bred and trained for profit, the cattle were used by the family and a few locals who stocked their freezer each year.

"You're looking real good, buddy. Try to keep your legs from bumping Cricket's sides."

"Like this, Daddy?"

"Yeah, Ty. Just like that."

Boone purchased the pony from a neighbor a few weeks before Jenny died. After Grace learned of the woman's prognosis, she'd jumped right in, making sure the older mare was ready for a young boy. When Jenny died, learning to ride had been good therapy for Tyler and a way for Grace to help Boone as he struggled with his new responsibilities.

Del reined up alongside them, nodding in approval at how well Tyler rode. "You're looking pretty good there, cowboy."

Tyler beamed at the compliment. "Thanks, Uncle Del. She likes me."

"Of course she does, Ty. You're a boy and she's a girl. It's the way things work," Boone said as he counted the cattle.

Del cleared his throat, making a decision before he could rethink it. "Amy and I are meeting Willow for dinner at Doc's Tuesday night." He knew Boone would find out anyway. Might as well get it out now.

Boone's jaw worked, his gaze focused straight ahead, as if he hadn't heard Del. Finally, he looked at his brother.

"Did she ask about me?"

Del shook his head. "Not exactly."

Boone snorted. "Yeah, I can imagine." He looked at his son. "Ty, why don't you ride over to Uncle Thorn while Uncle Del and I talk a bit."

Tyler wrinkled his nose. "More grown-up talk?"

"Afraid so."

Giving his pony the command, Tyler rode the short distance to Thorn. Boone watched, making sure his brother knew he had *Tyler duty*, then shifted his attention to Del.

"I haven't seen Willow since Jenny's memorial service. How's she doing?"

"You know Willow. She always seems to get along." Del knew that wasn't what Boone wanted to know.

"She's always been strong." Boone looked away, seeming to wrestle with what he wanted to say. Del let him work through his thoughts, not interrupting. "Did she mention anyone?"

"As in dating?"

"Yeah."

Del shook his head. "No. When I asked if she wanted to join us, she didn't even check her calendar. From what I've heard around town, she turns down anyone who asks her out."

This got Boone's attention. "Why would she do that?"

"I'm sure I don't know, but Willow must have her reasons. The only way to find out is to figure a way to get her to talk with you again."

"I've tried. She has no interest in anything I have to say, and I can't say as I blame her. After all that happened, how I acted..." He scrubbed a hand down his face. "It's best to leave it all in the past."

Del didn't agree, but it wasn't his decision to make. "You've got enough on your mind with Ty and the ranch. I just wanted you to know in case you decided to head to Doc's on Tuesday."

"I appreciate it, Del."

"I'm guessing you've never said anything to Thorn about what happened between you and Willow."

Boone shook his head, glancing over at his brother. He and Tyler were in deep conversation about something. Probably the lizard.

"I've been meaning to. Just haven't found the right time."

"Find the right time, Boone. It'll come out at some point, and it should come from you."

Chapter Two

"I'm so glad you invited me to join you." Willow sat across from Del and Amy, sipping a glass of wine, nodding at Mason and Lori, who sat at a table in the corner. She sagged back into her chair, her eyes showing fatigue.

"Sounds like you had a hard day." Amy rested a hand on Del's thigh.

"Not hard. Just long. One of the men out sick hasn't returned. I'm beginning to think he might be looking for another job." Willow shrugged, glancing around Doc's Grill and Tavern. "It isn't easy to keep good people. As soon as they're trained, they expect more money. I wish I could pay more, but it isn't possible most of the time."

Amy leaned forward. "I know what you mean. At Gray Wolf Outfitters, we lose people every week because they're moving, want more money, or believe they deserve a promotion. It seems everyone is looking for something they aren't getting."

"Are you happy there, Amy?" Willow asked, taking another sip of wine before setting her glass on the table.

"I love my job in purchasing. I talk to customers around the world, work with some wonderful people, and have good benefits. And I can walk to work. What's not to like?"

Willow blew out a breath. "Sounds wonderful."

Del's gaze narrowed on her. "You're not thinking of making a change, are you?"

Willow's brows shot up. "Me?" She shook her head. "Even if I wanted to, you know I can't. The Robinsons have owned the feed and tack store for three generations. My parents are retired and my brother is still in the army. There's no one else, and I won't be the one to sell."

Del glanced at Amy, keeping his reply to himself as Doc walked up.

"Your meals are almost ready, but I want you to try this new recipe." Doc set a plate containing samples in the center of the table. "My dear mama used to make her enchilada casserole at least twice a month when I was growing up."

Amy's eyes twinkled as she picked up her fork. "You've made some changes, of course."

A chuckle rumbled from Doc's throat. "Of course. Mama, God rest her soul, would forgive me if she knew."

"Hmmm. This is wonderful, Doc. What do you call it?" Willow took another forkful.

"Doc's Special."

Del shook his head. "You call all your new dishes Doc's Special. You need to get a little more creative."

"True." Amy nodded, taking another bite. "How about Mama's Special?"

"Or Mama's Enchilada Casserole?" Willow suggested, taking one more bite, then putting her fork down.

Scooping up the last piece, Del held it to his mouth. "Do any of these test dishes ever make it on the menu, Doc?"

Doc rubbed his jaw. "Well, that would mean printing a new menu."

"Sounds like a no to me." Amy picked up her soda, her eyes widening as the front door opened and Boone stepped inside, holding Tyler's hand. "Oh…"

"What?" Willow shifted to look behind her, color draining from her face.

Standing, Del walked to the front, his gaze locked on Boone.

"Uncle Del." Tyler ran up to him, finding himself lifted into his uncle's arms.

"What's up, buddy?"

"Daddy ordered pizza."

"Is that right?"

Tyler nodded. "Pepperoni."

Setting him down, Del looked at Boone. "Do you want to come over and say hello to Amy?"

Boone glanced at the table. He'd seen Willow the moment they walked inside, tensing at the way she tried to hide the contempt on her face. Shaking his head, he stepped up to the counter, taking out his wallet.

"I'd better not. Tell her I said hello."

"Look, Daddy. There's Aunt Amy."

Before Boone could stop him, Tyler dashed off, running up to give Amy a hug.

Del snickered. "I guess he made the decision for you."

Handing the money to the cashier, Boone picked up the box. "Am I mistaken, or are you enjoying this?"

Del's face sobered. "I know this is tough for you, and for Willow. Come over, say hello, then take Ty home." He tapped the box Boone held in his hand. "You have a good excuse not to stick around."

"Fine." Boone followed Del to the table. He leaned down to hug Amy, then his gaze moved to Willow, her features strained. "Hello, Willow."

Clearing her throat, she nodded. "Boone."

"Daddy got us pizza, Aunt Amy. Do you want some?" Tyler pointed to the box.

Smiling, she shook her head. "Knowing you and your dad, I don't think there's enough to share. Right, Boone?"

Pulling his gaze away from Willow, he shook his head. "Probably not. We'd best get going, Ty. You still have to eat and take a bath before going to bed."

"Can't we eat here?"

"Not tonight, buddy." Gripping the pizza box in one hand, he held out the other to Tyler. "Good to see you all. Enjoy your dinner."

Tyler waved as they walked away, Boone not looking back as they stepped outside.

Willow sat in her truck, gripping the steering wheel and taking slow breaths. Her appetite had fled the moment she saw Boone. Fighting the impulse to grab her purse and leave, she kept her seat, the stabbing pain in her chest almost overpowering.

Forcing herself to eat some of her meal, she stayed another thirty minutes, making small talk before asking the waitress to package her leftovers. Del had insisted on paying, then he and Amy walked her to her truck. No one had mentioned Boone after he left, although his presence seemed to hang over all of them.

A long time ago, Willow had accepted her responsibility for the way their relationship had ended and the resulting tragedy. He'd tried to be there for her, offering his support, imploring her to talk to him in all the phone messages, texts, and emails he sent. She'd ignored each attempt.

Her older brother, Greg, had been a rational sounding board. Besides Boone, Greg was the only other person who knew what had happened the night of the accident. To her surprise, he'd agreed to keep the circumstances from their parents, telling Willow the decision was hers to make. He'd also encouraged her to talk to Boone, get it all out, and come to some resolution so it wouldn't continue to haunt her. She refused to take his advice.

Years had passed since that night. After her refusal to speak with him, Boone had moved on, taking responsibility for Jenny's son. Willow had stayed frozen in time, wallowing in her pain.

Seeing him with Tyler, his obvious love for the boy, Willow's resolve to continue hating Boone dissolved. She knew they'd never reclaim any love they might have shared, but continuing to hate him did nothing except cause her more misery. Hanging onto the grief kept her from meeting anyone who might take Boone's place in her heart.

Starting the truck, Willow made a decision, one she'd been putting off far too long. She'd call Boone. If he still had the desire, which she hoped he did, she'd ask for a time they could talk. If all went well, she might be able to put the past behind her, walking away with a sense of peace she so desperately needed.

"One more, Daddy."

Boone held the book in his hand, watching as Tyler's eyes drifted shut and his breathing slowed. Most nights, two stories would do. Tonight, he'd read four before his son's voice dropped to a whisper.

My son. Boone still found it hard to comprehend the little boy, deep in sleep, was his. Most days went well. Some, like today, were more challenging.

He'd attended his first parent-teacher conference, learning Tyler sometimes showed signs of anger while on the playground. The teacher had called it *acting out*, his way of expressing the loss of his mother. Twice, he'd broken down. She'd found him crying in the corner of the playground. The day before, he'd shoved a couple boys after they'd called him names. All three had been sent to the principal's office.

Then, on the way home, a tire blew. Boone had forgotten to put an extra one in the truck, losing two hours waiting for roadside assistance and buying a replacement. Getting back on the road, he had no time to get to the ranch before having to return to school to pick up Tyler.

Somehow, he'd gotten the evening chores done before ordering pizza, forgetting Del and Amy were having dinner with Willow.

Setting the book down, he tucked the covers around Tyler, kissed him on the forehead, then crept from the room. Heading downstairs to the kitchen, he pulled a longneck bottle from the refrigerator, taking a long swallow.

Glancing at the clock, he blew out a breath. He needed to work on the ranch accounts before heading to bed, but his head wasn't into columns or numbers. All he could think about was Willow.

Boone hadn't spoken to her in so long, he'd almost forgotten the sound of her voice. Almost. Strong, throaty, with a silky edge. All it took was one word—his name—to bring back all the memories he so viciously shoved aside when she'd refused all his attempts at contact. At what seemed an all too common cliché, Boone hadn't realized what he had until he'd lost her.

Lowering himself into a chair, he picked up the controller. Burying himself in one of the sports channels or the one playing a constant stream of PBR competitions would relax him. With luck, it would also rid him of thoughts about Willow.

Tipping the bottle up, he drained the amber liquid, then pushed the button to recline the chair all the way back. Not much on tonight except a beautiful sports announcer interviewing another cocky athlete. Her long, dark auburn hair fell over her shoulders, soft blue eyes staring up at the man as he swiped moisture from his forehead. She looked so much like Willow, he had to shake his head. Blinking a few times, he looked again.

This time, the announcer had brown hair and dark brown eyes. *What the...*

Rubbing his eyes with the palms of his hands, Boone shook his head, then changed the channel to bull riding. Seeing Willow tonight was playing with his mind, the same as it had for a couple nights after he'd seen her at Jenny's memorial. He didn't look forward to pulling the covers up tonight only to fall into a fitful sleep filled with dreams of Willow.

He needed a good night's rest. Tomorrow was packed. After dropping Tyler at school, he'd have to hustle back to meet Mason, who was coming by to check one of the horses. Grace would arrive soon after to work with a new rider, a woman in her fifties who'd recently divorced and needed a diversion.

Boone could understand that. Perhaps he needed a diversion, too. Someone to take his mind off Willow. He couldn't remember the last time he'd met someone interesting and had a date, ending with a few hours in her bed. It had to be before he'd reconnected with Jenny and gotten involved in her life. As platonic as their relationship was, he hadn't had the urge to date. If not passionate, their time together had been filled with laughter, thoughtful discussions, and quiet evenings with Tyler. The hours he'd spent with her had meaning, much like the times he'd spent with Willow.

A familiar pang of regret squeezed his chest. He'd felt no desire for Jenny, only a deep friendship. Willow had been different.

They'd been friends since childhood. A tomboy, she always wanted to play with the Macklin and Taggert brothers, building tree houses, fishing, riding horses.

He remembered the time she'd tried to sneak onto the boy's little league team. She'd stuffed her hair into a baseball cap, pulled it low on her forehead, and worn something to hide her budding breasts. She'd stayed off by herself, appearing when the coach called for Will

Robinson. At first, the boys didn't recognize her. But with the first swing of the bat, Boone knew.

She'd been outed by one of the other boys, leaving with a red face but her head held high. He hadn't seen that Willow in a long time, and he missed her more than he could say.

A flash of a memory had him getting out of the chair and walking to the bookcase across the room. In a corner, behind a family portrait, he found what he sought. An old picture of a group of boys, all holding fishing poles in one hand, the fish they'd caught in the other. In the middle stood Willow. She had the biggest catch and the widest smile of the bunch. That girl sure did love to fish.

All those years, she'd fascinated him, made him smile. As they'd grown older, she'd made his head swim with her curves and beautiful smile. How had he not recognized his feelings for what they were? Could any man have been so blind?

Setting the picture back, he turned toward the stairs, certain of what he wanted to do. Before the week ended, he'd call Willow, invite her to come fishing with Tyler and him. He had nothing to lose. Certainly not her friendship.

He'd destroyed that a long time ago.

Chapter Three

Boone's week didn't improve after Tuesday.

Mason Taggert stopped by Wednesday morning to examine one of the horses. The diagnosis of laminitis didn't surprise Boone. Somehow, the horse had gotten into the grain storage, triggering the inflammation. Mason recommended cold packs, cold water hosing, and anti-inflammatory drugs. He also suggested corrective shoeing, which underlined the need for an experienced farrier. Mason gave Boone the name of one in Missoula and suggested calling his brother, Shane, for the name of a man he recently used.

Not long after Mason left, Grace showed up for her training session with a newly divorced woman with little riding experience. Selecting an older mare, one Boone had often used for new riders, Grace prepared for the lesson. Most students were expected to groom and saddle the horse before their session, then remove the saddle and groom the horse afterward. When the woman arrived, she made it clear she had no intention of doing anything except riding.

Calm under most circumstances, by the end of the hour, Grace told Boone she wouldn't be providing a second lesson. The woman complained about everything Grace recommended, didn't listen, and frustrated the mare. As much as they needed the income, Boone didn't argue, saying he'd post an ad on Robinson's bulletin board about lessons.

An hour after Grace left, the tractor broke down, stalling his work for the rest of the afternoon, until the time came for him to pick up Tyler.

Thursday hadn't been any better.

As he sat at the kitchen table Friday morning, Boone made a mental list of all he had to do. Take Tyler to school, stop by the principal's office, pick up the tractor parts he'd ordered Wednesday, meet Thorn for lunch, visit the bank, post the flyer Grace prepared at Robinson's. He stopped on the last.

Willow always worked on Friday afternoons. At least she had all the years he'd been going in there for supplies. And if he remembered right, Friday afternoons were slow, most customers trying to wind up their business earlier in the day.

Taking a sip of coffee, he winced, remembering he hadn't added sugar—a habit he'd started after high school when he needed the caffeine, hating the taste of the plain, black brew his father always made. After his parents died in a plane crash, he hadn't bothered breaking the habit, even with the purchase of a fancier machine and better grade of coffee.

Hearing footsteps on the stairs, Boone stood, grabbing a pan, eggs, and bread as Tyler bounded into the kitchen.

"Good morning, Ty." He glanced at him, seeing jeans, boots, and a plaid shirt tucked inside his pants, with a black leather belt. "You look good, son."

Tyler smiled, smoothing his hands down the front of his shirt. "I picked them out myself."

Boone smiled. "You did a real fine job."

Within minutes, he set a plate of scrambled eggs in front of Tyler, then poured a glass of orange juice. "Fifteen minutes before we have to be on our way."

Stuffing a forkful of eggs into his mouth, Tyler nodded. Leaning his hip against the counter, Boone watched his son, his heart squeezing. He wished he could speak with Jenny, ask her opinion on so many things. Most days, he got out of bed and felt adequate, doing the best he could without screwing Tyler up too much. Some days, he didn't feel even that level of confidence.

"Ready." Standing, Tyler put his plate in the sink, grabbed his backpack, and ran to the front door. "Are you coming, Daddy?"

Shaking his head, Boone grabbed his keys and hat, then followed his son outside. Fifteen minutes later, Tyler climbed out of the truck and waved goodbye, disappearing inside the school. A few minutes later, Boone sat in the principal's office, feeling the same sense of unease he had at Tyler's age.

"I understand Tyler lost his mother a few months ago." The principal leaned forward, clasping his hands together on the desk, a smirk on his face. "And you're his guardian, Mr. Macklin? Isn't that a little overwhelming to a single man?"

Boone had explained all of this to the original principal when he enrolled Tyler in school. Unfortunately, she had a family emergency, forcing her to take a leave of absence. Boone hoped she'd return soon.

"I am. Jenny, his mother, and I were friends. He has no other relatives."

The principal shook his head, snorting. "So you agreed to take custody?"

"Absolutely." No matter how inadequate Boone felt some days, he wasn't going to spill his uncertainties to anyone except his family. "I came in to let you know I spoke with Ty. He knows shoving the boys was wrong, but he also understands if he's bullied again, he's to tell me."

The man leaned closer. "We don't condone any type of violence, Mr. Macklin. If I hear of any, I'll call the police or the sheriff."

"I can understand that, but I want to be clear. I don't condone bullying and harassment. If you can't get those boys to stop, I'll call their parents and we'll work it out between us." Standing, Boone settled his hands on the desk. "Ty is a good boy, and I'm going to be an involved parent." Reaching into a pocket, he pulled out two business cards, setting them on the desk. "If there's a problem and you can't reach me, these are my brothers. They and their wives are on the list of those approved to speak on my behalf and take Ty home." Straightening, he walked to the door, opening it, then turned back to the principal. "I just want you to know I'm not alone in this. Ty has a whole family supporting him."

Closing the door behind him, Boone strolled out of the building. He'd met men like the new principal before. Smug, condescending, and self-righteous—all the qualities Tyler didn't need to learn at his age.

Climbing into the truck, he pulled onto the street, stopping to pick up the tractor parts he'd ordered, then made quick trips to the bank and dry cleaner. If he hurried, Thorn would be walking into Evie's Diner as Boone pulled into the parking lot. Patting his pocket, he felt the flyer Grace made up offering riding lessons. Robinson's would be his last stop.

"You have a call, Sheriff."

"Thanks, Bobby." Del took off his hat as he stepped into his office and closed the door before picking up the phone. "Macklin."

"Del, it's Nev McNabb."

Relaxing in his chair, Del grinned. "Hey, Nev. How're you doing?"

Neville McNabb was the sheriff in a neighboring county. A good man, one he could depend on if he ever needed help.

"Truthfully, I've been better. That's why I called."

Del sat forward, picking up a pen, then pulling a pad of paper out of a drawer. "Talk to me."

"Two children in the last three days have gone missing in my county. Girls. One age twelve and one fourteen."

"Same family?" Del asked.

"No. And these aren't cases of a divorced parent grabbing them. Mother and father are together in both families. The girls live about three blocks from each other."

"Amber alerts?"

"No. Other than the girls being missing, we don't have sufficient information for an alert. No make or model of a vehicle. No description of who may have taken them. I've got a friend with the FBI, but we have nothing to indicate they may have been taken over state lines." Nev blew out a breath. "Can I send you their descriptions?"

"Of course. I'll pass them around the office and give them to a detective I know on the local police force. I'm sure he'll get the word out, too. What else can I do?" Del read over his notes, setting down his pen.

"Nothing for now. I just wanted to let you know and ask you to be on alert. One family already has a private detective working for them. A little green, but she seems okay.”

“A woman?” Del asked.

“Last I checked. Anyway, I need to get going. I’ll send over what I have within the next few minutes.”

Del set the phone down, rubbing his chin. He knew drug smugglers used Montana to transport product between the United States and Canada. The northern part of the state was vast and sparsely populated, perfect for people wanting to move anything illegal between the countries. Like other states, Montana also had its share of human trafficking, much of it involving children and women.

Opening his email, Del saw the documents from Nev. He read through them, printing enough copies for everyone in his office, giving a set to each of his deputies, along with a brief explanation. Returning to his office, Del picked up the phone, dialing the local police department.

“Rick, it’s Del. Do you have time to talk?”

“Sorry I’m late.” Thorn slid into the booth opposite Boone at Evie’s Diner. “A new client came in and wanted to order a couple custom bikes. One for him and one for his son. Did you already order?”

"Just a couple sodas."

"Hello, boys." Evie walked up. "You're both looking fine today."

Thorn rested an arm across the back of the booth. "Okay, out with it, Evie. Are you looking for donations to the football boosters, science club, or…"

Grinning, she shook her head. "Can't a girl be nice and not be looking for something?"

"No," Thorn and Boone answered in unison.

"All right, you got me. We're having a fundraiser for the abused women's shelter." Reaching into her pocket, she pulled out four tickets. "Two each. Only $30 per ticket."

Thorn cocked his head to the side. "And?"

Evie huffed out a breath, looking between them. "Fine. How about gift certificates for motorcycle accessories at Scorpion and one riding lesson?"

"Done." Thorn reached into his pocket, pulling a hundred and twenty cash from his wallet. "For the tickets. I'll get you a gift certificate from the shop and have Grace make one up for an hour lesson. Now, can we order lunch?"

Snatching the money from Thorn's hand, she smiled. "Two cheeseburgers with fries. And yes, I know what each of you like on them." Turning on her heel, she walked behind the counter.

"Is it my imagination, or is Evie getting cockier in her old age?" Boone picked up his soda.

"Be careful, bro. She and I are the same age."

Lifting a brow, Boone tilted his glass toward his brother. "There you go."

Thorn grimaced, shaking his head. "And you owe me sixty bucks for the tickets. Now all you have to do is find some girl to go with you."

"And a babysitter." Boone picked up one of the tickets, checking the date. "It's over a month away. Plenty of time for me to find some unsuspecting woman and bring her along." He let out a breath, his mood sobering. "Do you have time to talk?"

Thorn's features stilled. "I always have time for you and Del."

Boone smiled, but it didn't quite reach his eyes. "And Grace."

"Well, yeah. I value my life. What's going on?"

"Here you are. Two cheeseburgers. Anything else?"

"This will do it, Evie. Thanks." Thorn waited until she'd walked back behind the counter, then looked back at his brother. "Talk."

Boone picked up his burger, took a small bite, then set it down. "It's about Willow."

"Okay. What about her?"

Scrubbing a hand down his face, Boone shook his head. "Maybe this wasn't such a good idea."

Thorn shook his head. "Let's have Evie wrap up our food and head to the park. This sounds like something that needs time and more privacy."

Fifteen minutes later, they sat on a park bench, unwrapping their food.

"When I first got back to town, I'd come here several times a week." Thorn chuckled. "Grace and I used to come here in high school. Anyway, one day Grace was here when I arrived. Turned out to be one of the best days of my life."

"You and Grace started seeing other again after that, right?"

"Close enough. Anyway, tell me what's going on with you and Willow."

"Nothing's going on now. It's about what happened a few years ago. I should've told you when you got out of the army, but there never seemed to be a good time."

Thorn held his hand up. "Does Del know?"

"I told him a few months ago, before Jenny died." Grabbing his drink, he gulped half of it down. "Del was running for sheriff and you were overseas when all this happened. Willow and I started seeing each other. I knew she loved me. Hell, I've always known how she felt, but I wasn't ready to accept it. We'd been seeing each other a few months when she stopped by one night." He glanced at his brother. "She was pregnant."

Thorn set down his burger, waiting for Boone to continue.

"I told her I'd marry her. You know, do the right thing. She, uh, asked if I loved her..." His voice trailed off, his mind going back to that night and the hopeful look on her face. "I told her I didn't. Willow told me to forget she came by. She'd rather be a single mother than live in a house with a man who didn't care." Shredding fingers through his hair, he leaned forward, resting his arms on his thighs. "She got into the truck and took off. A few miles down the road, a drunk driver crossed over the line, sending her truck into a ditch." Burying his face in his hands, he shook his head. "She lost the baby."

"Holy..." Thorn stood, pacing a few feet away before turning. "She blames you."

"Willow never said that, but I know she does. With all the privacy laws, she was able to keep it from her parents."

"Does Greg know?" Thorn knew Greg, Willow's brother, growing up. The same as Thorn, Greg had joined the army shortly after graduating high school.

"I don't know, but I think so. They were always tight, especially with their parents taking care of Greg's daughter when he's deployed."

Thorn sat back down, staring at the creek winding around the perimeter of the park. "Did you try talking to her after the accident?"

"I tried to get her to talk to me for months, but she never returned my calls. I went to her house, but she refused to open the door. When she returned to work, I tried to make an appointment to meet with her. Again, silence."

Nodding, Thorn clasped his hands together. "Why is it so important now? Does it have anything to do with Ty?"

"No." Boone stared into the distance. "Hell, I don't know. Maybe. All I know is I lied when I told her I didn't love her."

Thorn mumbled a curse. "You do love her?"

Boone glanced at him, nodding. "For a long time. For whatever reason, I could never admit it. Even when she told me about being pregnant. Why couldn't I have just told her? You did with Grace. Del did with Amy. What's wrong with me that I can't say the words?"

Thorn clasped him on the shoulder. "Nothing's wrong with you, Boone. You're one of the best men I know."

"Then why?"

"Are you asking for my opinion? Because that's all it would be."

"Your opinion would mean a lot to me."

Thorn looked away, his gaze following the stream. "I was a coward, not getting out of the service and coming back to the ranch to help you when the folks died. I know Del's work as a deputy kept him busy, which left you alone to run the ranch. You deserved better than me ignoring what you had to deal with back here. You were too damn young to have to handle it all alone."

Boone waved his hand in the air. "I made it fine."

"Did you? If I'd been here, would you have felt free to explore your feelings for Willow instead of spending time with various women, never forming any real relationships?"

"They were good women," Boone protested.

"Never said they weren't. But you never had the time for a personal life. Maybe when you and Willow did get together, you didn't know how to handle your feelings for her. You'd spent so much time on one-night stands with women you cared nothing about, you didn't know how to have a real relationship. Then you learned she was pregnant."

"I screwed it all up."

"What happened wasn't your fault, Boone. The drunk driver is the one to blame. My guess is you would've thought about it for a day or two, then gone to Willow and told her you loved her."

"You think so? Because I'm not sure."

"I know you, maybe better than you know yourself. You needed a little time to process it all. But yes, you would've asked her to marry you because you loved her, not because you felt obligated to do what was right."

Scrubbing both hands down his face. "If she'd just talk to me."

"Don't give her a choice."

Boone's brows furrowed, looking at Thorn as if he'd lost his mind.

"How badly do you want her?"

"It may have taken me a while, but I love her."

"Then do what's needed. Think about any time in your life when you wanted something bad enough to fight for it. What did you do?"

"Whatever it took."

Thorn settled an arm around Boone's shoulders. "Then there's your answer. Do whatever it takes to get her to talk to you. It can't be any more difficult than breaking a wild horse, right?"

Chapter Four

Willow bagged the items, handing them and the change to the customer. "Thanks. Hope to see you again soon."

"A new customer?" Deputy Bobby Baker stepped up to the counter, looking over his shoulder at the couple walking out the front door. The youngest of Del's deputies, he made it a point to stop in at Robinson's after lunch on Fridays.

Willow nodded. "Moved from California. I get a few new people each month. They don't buy much, but every dollar helps. Are you looking for anything specific today, Bobby?"

Crossing her arms, she leaned against the counter, her gaze moving to Tony Coletti in the tack section. From a longtime local ranching family, he was a Marine and one of Thorn's partners in Scorpion Custom Motorcycles. Even though the single women in town thought of him as a player, Tony was a genuinely nice guy, someone you could depend upon. He'd asked her out a couple times. She'd turned him down, and now regretted it.

Bobby rested a hand on his buckle, fidgeting with it. "Have you heard of the new dinner place in Falls Cave?"

Pulling her attention away from Tony, she shook her head. "Not a word. Have you been there?"

"Not yet. I was thinking of going this Saturday and wondered if you'd like to go with me."

Her eyes widened, a brow lifting. "Are you asking me on a date, Bobby Baker?"

Straightening, he nodded. "Yes, ma'am. I guess I am."

A smile tugged at the corners of her mouth. "You guess?" Her eyes darted to the front door, her breath catching when she spotted Boone walking inside. He headed straight toward Tony, not sparing her a glance.

"Willow, would you care to join me for dinner Saturday night?"

She didn't know much about Bobby, other than Del thought well of him...and the deputy was three or four years younger than her. If she ever planned to get her life back, stop staying home every night, she had to start somewhere.

"Yes, I think I would." Her smile grew when she saw the look of surprise on Bobby's face.

"Well, that's great. I'll, uh...how about I pick you up at seven?"

Picking up a pen and a piece of paper, she started to jot down her address.

"I know where you live, Willow." He shrugged at her pointed stare. "It's a small town. Being in law enforcement, I make it a point to know where most of the locals live."

She blew out a breath, her stomach churning. She'd just made a commitment to go out on a date. "Then I'll see you on Saturday." Willow almost laughed at the way

Bobby tripped over himself getting out of the store. It might not be her ideal date, but it was a start.

"Sonofa…" Tony's voice trailed off, his body going rigid when he felt a hand on his shoulder.

"Something bothering you, man?" Boone stood next to him, looking at what Tony held in his hand. "You don't like the brand, you can pick another."

"It's got nothing to do with this." He slid the item back onto the shelf. "I've been trying to get Willow to go out with me for months, with no luck. I just overheard her accepting a date with Bobby Baker."

A stab of jealousy ripped through Boone, knowing Tony had an interest in Willow and learning she'd accepted a date. "Del's deputy?"

"That's the one."

Boone's jaw clenched. "Bobby's still a kid. He must be four or five years younger than her."

Tony gave a disgusted nod. "That's what I figure. I gotta get back to the shop and regroup. Could be she's decided to start dating and Bobby asked first."

Boone glanced at Willow. "Yeah, maybe."

Tony shook his head, whatever he'd come in to buy forgotten. "See you later, Boone."

"See you, Tony." Boone didn't move, forcing himself to remember the reason he'd come into Robinson's. Thorn's words about doing whatever it took to get her to talk danced through his mind. If she was important enough to him, he had to make it happen.

Grabbing a couple items he didn't need from the shelf, he headed for the counter. For an instant, he felt certain she'd turn away, call someone from the back to ring him up. Instead, she lifted her chin, her hands gripping the edge of the counter.

"Hello, Boone."

Setting the items down, he reminded himself to relax. "Hi, Willow. Are you in here alone this afternoon?" He glanced around, aware of how quiet the store had become after Tony and Bobby left.

"It's almost closing, so I sent the guys home." Scanning the items, she gave him a total. "Do you want me to put this on your monthly tab?"

Reaching into his back pocket, he pulled out his wallet. "I'll pay with cash."

He took his time counting out the money, then handed it to her. That was when he noticed her shaky hand. Glancing up, he saw the drawn lines around her eyes and mouth, the wary expression.

"Here you go." She placed the change into his hand, and Boone swore he felt a surge of desire pulse through him.

Taking a quick look around, Boone forged ahead. "I've been thinking of taking Ty fishing this weekend. Maybe Sunday."

Her eyes lit up. "I'm sure he'd like that. He's five, right?"

"Six. We went one other time before his mom died and he caught on real fast."

Her face softened. "I've always loved to fish."

"Yeah, I remember. Any chance you'd want to come with us?" He held his breath as he watched a parade of emotions cross her face. Within seconds, he already knew she'd refuse.

Clearing her throat, Willow shook her head. "I'll be visiting my parents and Carly most of Sunday."

It wasn't a complete no. "How's Carly doing?"

"Good. She misses her dad. Greg calls when he can. He's supposed to be back in a few weeks."

Boone couldn't bring himself to give up and walk away. "How old is she now?"

The corners of Willow's mouth turned up. "Fourteen, going on twenty. She's started babysitting to earn extra money."

"Is that a fact? Maybe she'd want to watch Ty for me sometime." He noticed Willow stiffen the instant the words left his mouth.

"Must be hard for a bachelor like you to be tied down with a little boy on Saturday nights. It's got to mess with your sex life."

Feeling a prickle of irritation, he shook his head. "Being with Ty isn't a hardship, Willow. Once in a while, I'd like to meet Thorn and Grace or Del and Amy for dinner." He rubbed his chin, glancing down at the bag in his hand. "I can't remember the last time I had a date."

Biting her lip, she nodded. "Obviously before Jenny died."

Did she think he and Jenny had been in a relationship? Surely everyone in town knew they had just been friends.

"Jenny and I never dated. We hung out with Ty, kept each other company. Nothing more."

Her face flushed pink, which contrasted against her deep auburn hair. "I guess I thought, well...since you became Ty's guardian, I thought you and Jenny..." She looked away, unable to say more.

"Nope. Not ever."

She glanced at the front door at the sound of someone entering. "I'd better see to this customer. Thanks for the invitation to go fishing. Maybe some other time."

Definitely not a complete no. "Then you won't mind if I ask you again."

"I can't guarantee I can go, but you're welcome to ask."

Boone nodded, glancing at the clock on the wall behind Willow. "I'd better get going. Ty doesn't like it when I'm late picking him up. Have a good weekend."

"You, too." Watching him leave, she wished her feelings were different.

She didn't hate him. It would be easier if she did. Willow accepted she'd probably always be in love with him. She'd also accepted he'd never be in love with her. The worst part was, deep down, she knew being friends, spending time together, wouldn't make the ache in her heart go away.

They had so much in common, yet so little. She'd trust Boone with her life, but she'd never again offer him her heart. He'd already proven it wasn't of any interest to him at all.

Willow sat with her elbow on the table, chin in her hand, listening to Bobby talk about his job. He'd been going on for about fifteen minutes, unaware of her growing disinterest. The enthusiasm he had for his work and his respect for Del were obvious. And he had a good sense of humor. Unfortunately, her mind couldn't focus on the man across from her when it was filled with images of Boone.

She'd put off calling him all week, not knowing how to begin after so much time cutting him out of her life. Then she'd tossed aside the perfect opportunity to talk with her lame excuse of being with her parents and

Carly. She did have plans to meet with them mid-afternoon, leaving plenty of time to fish afterward or even before church. Willow still didn't understand why she hadn't seized the opportunity.

At least she'd gotten dressed up and out of the house. A good-looking young man, Bobby kept her entertained with stories from his high school days and working as a deputy. Too bad she simply couldn't stay engaged in the conversation.

Her mind couldn't let go of the brief moment speaking with Boone for the first time in what seemed forever. Although she'd felt a stab of pain when he walked up, the hurt had lessened as they spoke. Maybe that was what happened when enough time passed.

"Would either of you care for dessert?" The waiter handed them menus, listing the options.

Willow shook her head. "Nothing for me, thank you."

"I'll have a coffee and the check, please." Bobby looked at her. "You seem distracted. Is everything all right?"

She felt a pang of regret at Bobby's comment. He deserved to spend his time and money on a woman with a real interest in him, not a woman trying to get her social life back on track.

"I'm sorry, Bobby. I guess I haven't been the best of company."

He nodded at the waiter when he set down the coffee. "You've been fine, Willow. You just seem troubled by something."

"Not troubled. There's just a lot on my mind." Picking up her water glass, she took a sip, thinking of all she had to do. "I need to hire a couple more people, decide on a few new vendors, and sales aren't what they were a year ago. Nothing extraordinary. The usual problems faced by small businesses. And maybe the fact I haven't been on a date in a long, long time."

Bobby chuckled. "How long?"

She settled her hands in her lap, her brows scrunched together. "Close to three years. Sad, isn't it?"

"Hey, who am I to say? What's sad is a beautiful woman like you not getting out more. I know you've had plenty of offers."

Shifting in her chair, Willow shrugged. "I've been asked out. I just wasn't ready."

Taking a sip of coffee, he leaned forward. "I won't ask why. When you're ready, maybe someday you'll tell me."

"How do you know something happened?"

He lifted a shoulder. "A hunch."

Tilting her head to the side, she studied him. "It's what makes you a good deputy."

Bobby chuckled. "It's what *will* make me a good deputy. And learning from Del. He's a heck of a sheriff."

"I know. We're lucky to have him." Putting a hand over her mouth, she did her best to stifle a yawn.

"Appears it's time to get you home." Finishing the coffee, Bobby signaled the waiter, paying their bill. "Thanks for agreeing to have dinner with me."

"Thanks for inviting me. I did have a good time."

"So did I. Maybe you'll let me take you out again sometime."

Looking at him, a smile played across her face. "Maybe I will, Deputy Baker."

"Are we still going fishing tomorrow, Daddy?" Tyler sat cross-legged on the floor in front of Boone, who sat in a chair, working on a troublesome reel.

"We will if I can get this thing to work." Boone fiddled with the reel, then set it down. "I think it's good." Looking at the time, he stood. "Better get you to bed, buddy. We're going to start early."

Tyler jumped up, a smile on his face. "Are we going to miss church?" The hopeful look on the boy's face almost made Boone laugh.

"Afraid not. We'll be done in time to make the later service."

Tyler hung his head as he walked toward the stairs. "Oh."

Boone remembered feeling the same way when his parents herded him and his brothers into the truck every Sunday morning. Looking back now, it didn't seem as bad as what he thought when he was younger. Or maybe he'd mellowed over the years.

To his surprise, Tyler fell asleep after just one story. Boone knew he should head to bed himself, get a decent night's sleep. Walking downstairs, he made a cup of coffee, looking out the kitchen window.

He wondered how Willow's date with Bobby went and if they'd made plans to see each other again. The thought of her with someone else caused his throat to tighten, his chest to squeeze. It had taken him much too long to realize his feelings for Willow, refusing to believe he'd lost his opportunity.

Lowering himself into his favorite chair, Boone pulled out his phone. The impulse to call Willow, ask about her and Bobby, overwhelmed him. He'd dealt with the same urge for months after the accident.

He remembered feeling powerless when she refused to speak with him. After one short visit in the hospital, she'd asked him not to return. He'd honored her request, even though every instinct drove him to go back, do whatever was needed to get her to talk about what happened. Boone had shoved his own desires away. A week later, he learned she'd been released to go home.

No longer could he afford the luxury of giving her time. With her decision to date came an urgency he couldn't ignore.

His finger hovering over her number, he closed his eyes and touched it. After the fifth ring, her voice message came on. Boone hesitated a moment before ending the call and setting the phone down.

Rubbing his eyes with the palms of his hands, he let out a frustrated breath. He'd made progress with her, more than he dared hope. The fact she'd gone out with Bobby meant nothing.

If the look in her eyes and the flush of her cheeks when they spoke gave any indication, she still had feelings for him. Boone had no intention of giving up. He refused to let a future with Willow slip through his grasp a second time.

Chapter Five

Willow read the pages again, her eyes crossing. For the third time, she tried to complete another chapter in the mystery novel, unable to get past the first few pages. Setting the book down, she reached over, turned off the light, and pulled the covers under her chin.

She never needed warm milk, an herbal aid, or the television to get to sleep. Reading relaxed her, providing a gateway into peaceful slumber every night. The book failed her tonight.

Tomorrow, she'd go to church, return home to change, then drive to see her parents and Carly. The Sunday routine had become habit, one she looked forward to, until tonight. Boone's invitation to join them fishing added a twist to what had become a monotonous end to each weekend.

Willow loved her family, enjoyed spending time with them. She always came home in a good mood, selecting a movie to watch before reading her way to sleep.

So why couldn't she stop thinking about holding a fishing pole while spending time with Boone and Tyler? She already knew the answer. Being with Boone was toxic to her heart. For her own peace of mind, Willow needed to stick with her original plan, which meant never going out with him again.

Until yesterday, she never considered it a problem. He'd stayed away, giving her the space she insisted on after the accident. When he'd walked right up to her yesterday, spoken as if nothing of significance had happened between them, her defenses weakened. The invitation had caught her by surprise. At least she had the sense to turn him down. No good could come from an attempt at friendship, no matter the compelling assertions from her heart.

She enjoyed her evening with Bobby. Perhaps in time, it could grow into a friendship, or maybe more. Tonight had been a first step in moving forward, getting out of her rut and embracing life again. A step long overdue.

"That's it, buddy. Reel him in." Boone stood behind Tyler, encouraging him, while the young boy brought in his first trout. Leaning over, Boone grabbed the line, hoisting the fish onto the rocky shore. "Great job, Ty."

Removing the hook, Boone checked the size, then put it in the cooler filled with ice.

"You need to get one, Daddy. Want me to help you?"

Growing up the youngest of three boys, Boone had never suffered from a lack of advice. Between his father and brothers, he'd been given much more instruction than he ever asked for or wanted. Now Tyler wanted to do the same.

"Sure. I'll take all the help I can get."

By eight o'clock, they had five fish, plenty for the two of them. Loading the gear into his truck, they made the short trip home, arriving in time to clean the fish, take showers, and get to church.

The worship service had started by the time Boone hustled Tyler into a pew near the back. Picking up a hymnal, Boone opened to the page shown on the big screen at the front of the church. They usually sat with his family closer to the front.

When the singing ended, Tyler and the rest of the children left to attend Sunday school, leaving Boone sitting alone at the back, a location he preferred. It gave him time to think—sometimes about the sermon, sometimes about other things. Today, his mind immediately went to Willow.

"Mind if we join you?"

Boone looked up to see Mr. and Mrs. Robinson, Carly, and standing a few feet behind them, Willow.

Sliding over, he motioned to the empty space next to him. "Please."

"I don't know how we got here so late. Seems if you get up at dawn you could get to church on time." Mrs. Robinson gave her husband, who slid in next to her, a pointed stare.

Patting his wife's knee, Mr. Robinson smiled, glancing at Boone. "Got caught up in a project."

"Can you move farther down?" Willow stood in the aisle, the last to be seated.

"Go on around, sweetheart, and sit next to Boone. You know how Carly likes to be on the aisle."

Willow's gaze narrowed on her father for an instant before she nodded, doing as he asked. After a lousy night where she'd gotten little sleep, now she had to sit next to the man who'd been the reason for her exhaustion.

"Good morning, Willow."

She barely glanced at him. "Boone."

He didn't give her too much space, causing their legs to touch when she sat down.

"Can't you move down any farther?"

He motioned to her mother on the other side of him, indicating the lack of room. "Sorry. This is the best I can do." When she bit her lower lip, Boone leaned toward her. "I don't bite, Willow."

She shot him a disbelieving look. "I happen to know you do," she hissed, turning to face the front.

He winced at the retort, not missing her meaning. The comment brought back memories he didn't want to think about in church.

Opening the program, Willow feigned interest in every line, including the identical announcements included every week.

Boone kept glancing over at her. He didn't want to make her uncomfortable, but he couldn't lose this opportunity to talk to her.

Somehow, he needed to take the first step in healing the fissure he'd created, apologize for his part in the accident. If she then chose to turn away, have nothing more to do with him, he'd accept it, even though he wouldn't like it.

Turning his attention to the man at the pulpit, Boone forced himself to focus on the message. Forgiveness was this morning's theme. Asking for it, giving it, and accepting it. The minister covered the subject in detail, providing answers before anyone could formulate their questions.

One of the reasons Boone liked the minister was the informal gatherings after service. Those who attended church were invited to stay, ask questions about the message. As many as a dozen people would stick around. Before Jenny's death, Boone had stayed a couple times, trying to make sense of the impending death of a vibrant, young woman. He never quite got there, but along the way, discovered an appreciation for the dedication of the minister. He was the main reason Boone came as often as he could.

The sound of music dragged his attention back to the service and the woman next to him. Looking over, he saw Willow's eyes locked on him before she shifted her gaze to the front.

Leaning toward her, he lowered his voice, ignoring the knot of unease in his gut. "Have dinner with me."

Her lips parted, but she didn't speak. Instead, she shook her head.

"Then lunch or coffee. Whatever is convenient for you."

Mrs. Robinson touched his arm. "The minister is speaking again, Boone."

Wincing, he leaned away from Willow.

When the service ended, he followed her outside, touching her shoulder when she started toward her car.

"Willow...stop."

She took a couple more steps, then slowed, turning toward him. Crossing her arms, she looked at him. "What do you want from me, Boone?"

"A conversation. That's all I want. All I've ever wanted since the night you walked out."

Closing her eyes, she stared down at the ground, letting out a deep breath. "If you want to know if I blame you, I don't."

"You don't have to, Willow. I blame myself." Placing a finger under her chin, he lifted her head until she looked at him. "I shouldn't have let you leave that night."

Stepping back, she wrapped her arms around her waist, shaking her head. "You couldn't have stopped me, Boone."

"You were upset. I should've tried harder to make you stay."

"It wouldn't have mattered." Blinking a few times, she did her best to hide the moisture in her eyes. "I need to leave." Turning toward her truck, she stopped when Boone gripped her arm.

"Have dinner with me, Willow."

Letting out a shaky breath, she shook her head. "I don't know what you want from me."

Boone's gaze searched hers. "Nothing, except a few minutes of your time. I'm not asking for anything more from you."

Willow knew he was right, pushing her to talk. She'd planned to call him and do the same, but she couldn't find the courage. He'd always had more guts than her.

"Coffee."

He nodded. "When and where?"

Glancing around, she swiped hair off her face. "Tuesday morning, but not at Evie's. I don't want her jumping to any conclusions about us."

"Doc will let us into his place."

"But he doesn't offer breakfast."

Boone grinned. "He will for us."

"Thanks for seeing me, Del." Burnt River Detective Rick Zoeller handed him a cup of coffee from Evie's before sitting down, looking around the office. "I see you haven't changed anything since the last time I visited."

Chuckling, Del looked at the almost blank walls, stacks of paper on his desk and file cabinet. "Maybe I should get Amy in here to help me out."

"Couldn't hurt." Rick took a sip from his cup, his grin disappearing. "We need to talk."

"About what?"

"You know the call you got from Nev McNabb about the abducted girls?"

Leaning forward, Del rested his arms on the desk. "What about them?"

"I called a few colleagues. Seems we may have an epidemic on our hands." Reaching into his pocket, he pulled out a small notepad. "Five girls between eleven and fifteen have gone missing around Missoula in the last month. Six from the Billings area. Two from a small town named Splendor, which is north of here." He glanced up. "You remember Pierce O'Brien?"

Del nodded. "Of course. Your friend from the Coeur d'Alene Police Department."

"He knows of four girls missing from towns in that area. All within the last thirty days, all under the same circumstances."

Picking up his coffee, Del took a sip, then grabbed a pen and paper. "Tell me about the circumstances."

Rick stared down at his notes. "Pretty simple. Each girl was alone. Walking home from school or a friend's house. One was sitting on a bench in the park, away from all the other kids and families. All were taken between four and eight at night." Closing the notepad, he looked up. "Not one single witness for any of the abductions."

Del's brows furrowed. "How can that be? Someone must have seen something."

"You'd think, but according to reports, no one saw a damn thing."

"What about the girl in the park?"

Rick shook his head. "A couple remember seeing her when they walked by. They sat down maybe fifty yards away, talked for a while, then heard a scream. They ran in the direction of the scream, but when they got there, the bench was empty. Not long afterward, her parents reported her missing. The couple identified her from a photo."

"Professionals?"

Rick nodded. "That would be my guess. An organized ring of child traffickers. State and federal agencies are on it, but manpower is limited. I haven't been able to talk to anyone who's tied them all together. One of my contacts believes they're being categorized as random abductions of opportunity, not connected to one organization."

"You don't buy it." Del tossed down his pen.

"All I know is there are a lot of girls being taken within a few hundred miles of Burnt River. The rest I'll leave to those doing the investigating."

Del stood, picking up the cup, leaning a hip against the edge of his desk. "What do you suggest?"

"I think we need a local task force to come up with a plan, including making people aware of what's going on."

Del finished the coffee, tossing the empty cup into the trash. "The mayor will never agree if it causes a panic or hinders what little tourism the town has."

"Then we need to come up with a plan he can accept that still puts the people on notice. You have his ear, Del. You could explain the situation."

Snorting, Del sat back down. "The mayor tolerates me, Rick. He pushed for the other candidate."

"Who has his ear?"

Del pinched the bridge of his nose, then sat back. "Wolf Jackson."

"The chairman of Gray Wolf Outfitters?"

"The same. He and the mayor go way back, the same as my father and the mayor—when my father was alive. The mayor respects Wolf."

Rick nodded. "And Wolf respects you."

"And as you know, his daughter, Grace, is married to Thorn. She loves children and is going to school to get a degree in education. We should bring her in on this. Wolf will do just about anything for her."

Rick rubbed his chin. He and Grace had gone out a few times before she and Thorn reconnected. He'd always been impressed with her. "Having civilians in on this could be tricky. But if it accomplishes our goal, I'm all for it. Anybody else outside law enforcement we could bring in?"

"Either Shane or Mason Taggert. They're respected and know most of the people in the area. Maybe Doc Stone. I'll need to think on it a little."

Standing, Rick slid the notepad back into his pocket. "I haven't gone to the chief on this yet. It might be better coming from you."

Del understood his point. In most everyone's eyes, he and the police chief were considered equals. "Another man who isn't overly fond of me, but that's never stopped me from pushing for what I think is right."

"Rumor around the station is the man may not run again. He might retire after this term."

Del cocked his head, raising a brow. "That's news to me."

Resting his hand on the back of the chair, Rick shook his head. "Word has it he's been diagnosed with cancer. Possibly inoperable."

"Geez, that's tough. I don't care for the man, but I wouldn't wish that on anyone."

"Yeah." Rick walked to the door, opening it. "I'd better get back. Thanks for the help on this. I'm hoping to get something going by the end of the week."

Watching Rick leave, Del looked at his calendar. It was already Monday morning. He'd better get hustling if he wanted to contact the right people and get their support before he approached the mayor.

Boone watched as Tyler walked into the school, feeling the usual pang of emotion. He'd never expected to love the boy this way, as a real father would. The truth was he'd do anything for Tyler, give his life, if needed. The notion surprised him. So much had changed in so little time.

Driving back home, he thought of tomorrow and coffee with Willow. Boone felt like a kid on his first date, except he didn't expect this to go so well. There wouldn't be any goodbye kisses or warm hugs.

They'd be talking about some tough stuff, painful to both of them. She might even get up and walk out. He had no idea what to expect and couldn't guess at an outcome.

Pulling into his driveway, he cut the engine as his phone rang. "Hello."

"Boone. It's been a long time, bro."

A grin spread across Boone's face. "This sounds like Kell. But that can't be because the last I heard, he's on some secret assignment somewhere in the Middle East."

Kell's chuckle came through the phone. "Damn straight I was. I'm back now and looking to hang for a few nights. You game?"

"You bet. Where are you, man?"

"I'll be in Burnt River on Thursday. Hoping I can stay at your place a few nights."

"You know you're always welcome, Kell." Boone's enthusiasm faded a little when he remembered Tyler. "Uh, there's one little detail, though."

"Yeah? What's that?"

"If we're going out, I'll need to locate a sitter."

The silence had Boone wondering if Kell heard him. "As in a babysitter, Macklin?"

"That would be the kind. You've been gone a while. We've got a lot to catch up on." He heard Kell snort on the other end.

"Seems we do. I've gotta go, but I'll see you Thursday afternoon. And keep this number. It's new." Kell hung up before Boone could respond.

Getting out of the truck, he slid the phone into his pocket, the smile still on his face. He and Kellen Brooks had been friends since first grade, causing more trouble than he cared to remember. Now he saw him maybe once every couple years when Kell was home from assignment.

Bounding up the steps to the front door, Boone walked inside, already running through a mental list of who might be able to watch Tyler for a couple nights. Del and Thorn for sure, but after that, he had no one. Well, he had a few days to come up with someone.

They'd probably make dinner and hang at the ranch Thursday night, give Kell a taste of what fatherhood would be like if he ever took the plunge. Most likely, they'd go out Friday and maybe Saturday. Once word spread about Kell being back, there'd be plenty of old friends to keep him company.

Boone grabbed his work gloves and headed outside, feeling a little lighter than he had in a while. It would be good to see a friendly face. Yep, darn good.

Chapter Six

Willow turned off the engine, making no move to get out. Other than her truck and the one she recognized as Boone's, there were just three other vehicles in Doc's parking lot. At least they'd have a lot more privacy than at Evie's.

She checked herself in the mirror, feeling a little foolish to worry about her appearance. Boone didn't care what she looked like. His only reason for insisting they meet was to clear his conscience—the same reason she'd agreed to see him. Willow needed to clear her own.

Getting out, she walked around to the front, seeing Boone through one of the large windows. He spotted her right away, lifting a hand in greeting before standing. By the time she walked to the table, he had pulled out her chair, a cup of coffee already waiting for her.

"I wasn't sure you'd come."

Sitting down, she hooked her purse over the back of the chair. "I would've called if I couldn't make it. Besides, it's time we came to some kind of understanding about the past."

"Understanding?" Boone asked, tilting his head to the side.

She let out a frustrated breath, picking up her coffee. "Clear the air." Taking a sip, she set the cup down. "I didn't handle things well after the accident, and for that, I'm sorry."

Leaning forward, Boone cradled his cup with both hands, rolling it between them. "There's nothing to apologize for. You were going through a tough time. It couldn't have been easy deciding not to tell your parents about the pregnancy. I wish you would've let me help."

"You tried several times to talk and I ignored you. I'm ashamed of how I treated you." Shaking her head, she looked down at her trembling hands.

Reaching across the table, he laid a hand on top of hers. "Don't be. Neither of us handled it well." Boone swallowed the lump in his throat. "It should never have played out the way it did."

Both quieted at the sound of footsteps coming toward them. "Doc asked me to see if you wanted more coffee." The young woman held up the pot in her hand.

Boone nodded, lifting his cup. "Thanks."

She filled both cups. "We have sweet rolls in the back. Would you like some?"

Willow shook her head. "Not for me, thank you."

"I'm good. Does Doc need us out of here by a certain time?" Boone asked, adding sugar to the coffee.

"He wanted you to know you can stay as long as you want. The lunch crowd starts arriving a little before noon. I'll be in the back if you need anything else."

Once she disappeared into the kitchen, Boone cleared his throat. "I know you have no reason to reconsider us, Willow, but that's what I'm asking."

Her lips parted, a whoosh of breath escaping. "*Us?*"

"Yes, us." He sat back, his hands resting on the tabletop. "I want to try again. What happened the last time, well...I wasn't ready. When you told me you were pregnant, I said all the wrong things. I realized it not long after you left that night." A haunted look crossed his face. "By then, it was too late."

Willow's eyes began to blur, her mind fogging at his request. She'd never considered he might want to try again. After all, he'd been clear he didn't love her. Clasping her hands together, she shook her head.

"It wouldn't work, Boone. I've come to accept we just aren't meant to be."

Leaning forward, he noticed the slight tick at the corner of her eye. It told him more than her words. "Is that what you believe or what you want to believe?"

Her heart tripped in her chest as she considered his question. The answer was simple. "It's what I know to be true. You don't love me. You never have and never will. It took me a long time and a lot of introspection to admit it, but no matter what I did, how much I loved you, it would never be enough. I'm not *the one*, Boone." A sad smile curved the corners of her mouth. "You deserve to be with a woman who means everything to you. A woman you think about the instant you wake up and as you drift off to sleep. I'm not that woman." Pushing the cup away, she started to stand.

"Stay, Willow. Please."

She didn't want to hear any more. Leaving now would be no better than what happened after their last confrontation. She'd run, and it hadn't turned out well. Lowering herself back into the chair, Willow clasped her hands together.

"Thank you." Boone had no idea where to go from here, except to be honest. "When you told me about being pregnant, I panicked. I'd taken responsibility for the ranch not long before we got together. With Del working more than full-time as a deputy and Thorn overseas, I had little support, no backup plan if stuff went wrong." His jaw worked, his mind going back to their time together before the accident. "Being with you turned out to be the best part of every day. I could relax, let my worries about the ranch fade away, and be myself. I'd never been that way with anyone else, not even my brothers. But love..." Boone shook his head. "Honestly, I hadn't given it much thought. I was twenty-four and unprepared for the hard choices that came with a family, Willow. At least that's what I believed when you said we were having a baby." His chest squeezed when he thought of how old their child would be if the accident never happened. "I didn't respond well, and for that, I'm sorry."

Looking down at her hands, she shook her head. "None of it was your fault, Boone."

"After the first few weeks, I didn't use a condom. It was selfish and immature."

Willow's features softened. "We talked about it. I was on the pill and had been for a few years. We thought it was enough." The day she'd gotten the results of the pregnancy test, she didn't think it through before driving to the Macklin ranch. "I should've waited to tell you. You'd already called to tell me about the mare and foal Dr. Johnson couldn't save. I knew their deaths crushed you, but I was too selfish to let your feelings get in the way of giving you the news."

Boone remembered how he felt when the vet shook his head, letting him know they were both gone. He'd put so much hope on the mare and what would've been a beautiful colt. He hadn't been at all receptive when he learned about the pregnancy. Still, he wondered when he would've been.

"It wouldn't have mattered when you told me, Willow. For the first few years, every day was a struggle to keep the ranch solvent. Until recently, I always felt the hammer could come crashing down at any moment, forcing me to sell."

"Which you never would've done."

He choked out a harsh laugh. "Probably not." Swallowing the last bit of coffee, he set the cup aside. "What do you say, Willow? Can we try it again?"

Her gaze darted around the room, as if she fought for the right response. "I don't know, Boone. You didn't love me before. If I've learned anything, it's that you can't force someone to love you." When he opened his mouth to respond, she held up a hand. "Maybe we can be friends."

"Friends?" The word tasted bitter on his tongue.

"You know...not ignore each other when you come into the shop, sit together at church sometimes, go fishing." Her eyes sparkled on the last.

She offered something he could work with. "Maybe take Ty for pizza and ice cream."

Chuckling, she nodded. "Maybe."

"If that's what you can offer, I'll take it."

Pushing back her chair, she stood, extending her hand. "Friends."

Boone smiled, gripping her hand. "Friends."

Her hand in his felt like much more than friendship, but he wouldn't mess up the new arrangement. He had time, and for now, it was enough.

"Sorry, Boone. Amy and I are having dinner with Ashley and Josh tomorrow night. Have you tried Thorn and Grace?"

"Tried them first, Del. Don't worry about it. I'll figure something out. Are you still coming out Saturday?"

"Same as always. Have coffee ready this time."

Boone could hear the humor in Del's voice. "Will do. And Kell is staying with me, so he'll be helping out."

"That's who you're going out with Friday night? I thought you had a date."

"Not yet, but I'm hopeful. I'd better get busy and see who I can find to watch Ty. See you Saturday, Del." Hanging up, Boone ran a hand through his hair, trying to come up with anyone who might babysit Tyler.

Opening the contacts on his phone, he started scrolling through them, stopping on Willow. Not wanting to push her, he'd avoided calling the last two days. With Kell coming into town this afternoon, Boone thought it best to wait until after the weekend. The corners of his mouth tilted upward. Now he had a good excuse to call.

Touching the button, he leaned back in the chair, his heart rate rising as he waited for her to answer. After several rings, he expected it to go to voicemail. Instead, she picked up.

"Boone?"

"Yeah. Did I interrupt anything?"

"Working on inventory, so any interruption is welcome. Do you need something?"

"Not from the store. This is a personal call." Boone tapped his fingers on the arm of the chair, waiting to see if she'd make some excuse and hang up.

"Okay..."

The knot in his stomach tightened. "I'd like to see about you joining me and Ty for fishing. Not this weekend, but the following Saturday. I have plenty of gear and bait. What do you say?" He held his breath, waiting.

"Only if you let me bring the food."

He blew out the breath he'd been holding. "No arguments on that. I'll call you next week to set it all up."

"Sounds good. If that's all, I should be getting back to the inventory."

"There is one other thing. I, uh…need a babysitter on Friday night. Do you think Carly would be interested?" As soon as the words were out, he realized how it sounded. "It's not for a date, Willow. Kell Brooks is coming into town today. I thought we'd go to Kull's, see some of our friends from school. You're welcome to join us."

"You don't have to explain your personal life to me, Boone. What you do and who you date are none of my business."

Scrubbing a hand down his face, he shook his head. "You're right. Just wanted to clarify why I wanted to talk with Carly." Again, he waited, hoping he hadn't blown it.

"I'm sure she'd love to watch Ty. You can call her. She'll be home from school after three."

"Thanks, Willow. And don't change your mind about fishing. I'm counting on that food you promised." Hearing her chuckle, he began to relax.

"I won't change my mind, Boone."

"Good. And think about joining us tomorrow night at Kull's. Six o'clock. We'll have a few drinks, then head over to Doc's for dinner."

"I'll think about it. No promises, though."

"Sure. Hope to see you tomorrow."

Hanging up, he slumped back in the chair, a grin on his face. Even if she didn't show tomorrow night, he'd made progress. In a week, he'd be spending the morning fishing with Willow. Something he never thought he'd do again.

Kell sat on the porch, a beer in his hand, watching Tyler chase Boone around the yard. After the last few missions, anything approaching a normal life made him feel human again.

Boone didn't know it, but Kell might not be heading back. He'd been ordered to take time off, get his head together, then go through a series of psych reviews before a decision would be made about returning to duty. The thought of not going back to his team frightened him. The possibility of a civilian life scared the hell out of him.

"Come on, Uncle Kell." Tyler waved at him, doubling over in laughter when Boone picked him up, spinning him around.

"Yeah, Uncle Kell. You're missing all the fun." Boone carried Tyler to the porch, setting him on a chair next to Kell. "I'm going to grab a beer. You want another?"

Kell nodded as he drained the last of what was in the longneck, watching as Tyler began to settle down.

"Daddy says I get to have a babysitter tomorrow night."

Kell stretched out his long legs, crossing his ankles. "Is that so?"

Nodding, Tyler sat up in the chair, his expression somber. "Her name is Carly and she's a girl."

Steeling his features so as not to laugh, Kell nodded. "Makes sense. Do you like girls?"

Shaking his head, he slid off the chair. "They do weird things. Daddy says I won't think they're weird in a few years, but I think I will. Girls don't like lizards."

"I didn't know that."

Pursing his lips, Ty shook his head. "They don't. Daddy let me take mine to school for sharing and all the girls screamed. The next day, I had to let him go because Daddy said they aren't meant to be caged. But it wasn't a cage. It was a box, so I don't think Daddy was right."

"What was I wrong about?" Boone stepped outside, handing an orange juice to Tyler and a beer to Kell.

"The lizard was in a box, not a cage."

Taking a long swallow, Boone nodded. "Ah, the box versus cage discussion. Either way, you couldn't keep him, Ty. If my mom were alive, she'd tell you the same."

Tyler's eyes widened, his mouth opening. "You had a mommy?"

Kell burst into laughter, spewing the beer in his mouth across the porch.

Boone glared at him. "It isn't that funny."

"The hel…I mean, the heck it isn't." Kell looked at Tyler. "You sure are a smart kid."

Tyler grinned. "That's what Daddy says." Looking at the driveway, he ran to the edge of the porch, pointing at a car driving up. "Who's that?"

Stepping beside Tyler, Boone squinted, trying to get a better look inside the sleek sports car. He mumbled a curse when the doors opened.

"Who is it?" Kell asked, setting his beer down to join them. "Well, what do we have here?" Walking down the steps, his smile broadened at the sight of two women coming toward him.

"Hey, Kell. We heard you were in town and thought we'd come out to welcome you." A curvy brunette walked up, slipping an arm through his. Standing on tiptoe, she planted a kiss on his cheek.

"Sarah Mae. It's been a long time, darlin'. It's good to see you." Kell wrapped an arm around her waist, pulling her to him. "And who is this?"

"This is my cousin, Bethany. She drove all the way over from Billings to meet you."

"All the way from Billings, huh? Well, it's nice to meet you, Bethany." Slipping his other arm around her waist, he turned toward the porch. "Guess we'll need a couple more beers."

Boone felt a tug on his pants and looked down. "Who are they, Daddy?"

Letting out a sigh, Boone plastered on a smile. "Just a couple friends, son. Come on. I'll introduce you."

So much for a kickback evening with Kell. The girls stayed for hours, drinking beers, sharing the steaks Boone marinated. Tyler seemed fascinated by the two women, neither looking anything like his aunts, Grace and Amy. Tight, short dresses, four-inch heels, and enough makeup to last most women a year, they laughed at everything the men said. Kell seemed to be having a good time. All Boone wanted to do was hit the sack.

He'd gone out with Sarah Mae a few times. It had been a few years, but it didn't take long to remember why four dates had never gone to five. Dumb as a post was what Del had called her after he joined them at Kull's one evening. Back then, Boone wasn't going out with her for her mind. Watching her now, he winced, wondering why he wasted even four nights with her.

She wasn't all that bad. She just wasn't Willow.

"I'd better get Ty to bed. He's got school tomorrow." Walking to the sofa, he scooped the sleeping boy into his arms, sensing a presence next to him.

"Do you want some help tucking him in?" Sarah Mae's slightly slurred voice irritated him. He knew what she was asking.

"Nah, I've got him." Stopping at the foot of the stairs, he turned back toward her. "You know, I have an extra bedroom down the hall with two beds. Maybe you and Bethany should consider crashing here."

Swaying toward him, she touched his arm. "I'd rather share your bed."

"Sorry, Sarah Mae. That's not going to happen." Boone didn't wait for her to reply before climbing the stairs.

Tucking Tyler in, he sat beside him longer than necessary, watching the boy sleep. Whoever his father was must've been a real piece of work. Boone couldn't imagine walking away from such a gift, missing out on the joy Tyler brought to everyone. Stroking his hair, he leaned down, dropping a kiss on his forehead, then stood. Time to either sober the girls up or move them to the guest bedroom.

Walking down the stairs, the first thing he noticed was the quiet. Freezing at the bottom of the steps, he looked around, surprised to see the living room and kitchen were empty. He sure hoped Kell hadn't decided to invite them both to stay in his room. That simply wouldn't work with Tyler in the house.

He should've known his friend had more sense than that. Laughter drew Boone to the front porch, a weary smile crossing his face seeing Kell help them into their car. Stepping away, Kell waved as they drove off.

"I forgot about you and Sarah Mae. She sure was miffed when you turned her down tonight." Kell joined Boone on the porch.

"They okay to drive?"

"Yeah. They didn't have as much as they wanted us to think. I made them each coffee before sending them on their way." Kell dragged a hand down his tired face. "Guess I'm getting old."

Boone turned to look at him. "How's that?"

"I'd rather have a cup of coffee out here on the porch with you than have either of them in my bed. Pathetic, isn't it?"

Boone clasped him on the back. "Not at all, bro. I think we're just growing up."

"Ah, hell, man. That sounds even worse."

Boone had to agree, but for some reason, it didn't bother him like it used to. "How'd you get them to leave?"

Scratching his chin, Kell winced. "Told them we'd be at Kull's tomorrow."

"Ah, hell," Boone mumbled as he entered the kitchen.

"Sorry, man. Guess we're looking at round two."

Chapter Seven

"Come on in, Carly." Boone's smile widened when he saw Willow get out of her truck and walk up the steps. "I didn't know you were bringing her."

Shrugging, Willow followed Carly inside. "Made sense. If the offer is still open, I decided to stop by Kull's for a little bit, visit with Kell. I'll come back here later to pick up Carly."

Closing the door behind them, Boone saw Carly already on the floor next to Tyler, playing with his newest monster truck. "You brought her here, so I'll take her home."

"If you're sure, that would be great." Her attention moved to Tyler, whose animated movements and sound effects already had Carly laughing. "He sure is a handsome little boy," she mumbled, more to herself than anyone else.

Shoving his hands into the pockets of his jeans, Boone nodded. "He is. And much too smart for me. It's a struggle to keep up with all his questions...and his energy. Ty never stops. He's on the go from the time he wakes up until he collapses onto his bed," he chuckled.

"Thought I heard voices down here." Kell walked up to Willow, wrapping her in a tight hug. "It's been a while."

Keeping her arms around him, she looked up. "Too long, Kell. When are you going to get out and move home?" Dropping her arms, she stepped away.

"That's the big question. Someday, I'll spend time thinking on it. For now, it's just good to be back." Kell looked at Tyler, then moved his attention to Boone. "I'm telling you, though, it was a shock to learn my main man is a father."

Her lips tilted into a grim smile. "You weren't the only one. I don't think anyone saw it coming. It seems to be working out all right." She cast a look at Boone, who crossed his arms and shrugged.

Kell nodded toward Carly. "So that's Greg's daughter."

Willow quirked an eyebrow. "You've never met her?"

"Nope. I haven't been back in a while. Last time, Greg was out on one of his missions. How old is she?"

"Fourteen." She pressed her lips together.

"When's he due back?" Boone asked.

"It's anyone's guess. We'll know when he calls us from base." She crossed her arms, her back stiffening, a clear indication of her frustration.

Kell placed a hand on her shoulder. "I know it's hard for families. My parents go through the same. As soon as I get back, I always stop by to see them for a few days."

She nodded. "I heard they moved somewhere a little warmer. Arizona?"

"A couple hours north of Phoenix. They get a little snow, but nothing like around here. Mom loves it."

"And your father?"

His face split into a wide grin. "He loves whatever Mom loves."

Boone stood a few feet away, watching Carly and Tyler interact while listening to Kell and Willow. Their easy banter made him feel a little out of place, as if he could leave and neither would notice. He knew it was a ridiculous thought, shaking his head to shove it aside.

"You ready, old man?" Kell chuckled when Boone shot him a disgruntled look.

"Give me a minute with Carly."

Kell slung an arm over Willow's shoulders. "We'll meet you outside."

Boone bit back a retort. Kell was almost like a brother. Neither would go after a woman the other had his sights on. After working together on the ranch most of the day, Kell knew Boone's intentions toward Willow. His friend's actions now were pure show, meant to rile Boone into action. And they were working.

After giving Carly a brief tour, reviewing the contents of the refrigerator, providing her his cell number and Kell's, and showing her the emergency contact list, he grabbed the keys to his truck.

"Call with any questions, Carly." His nervous gaze landed on Tyler, who'd barely looked up since he started playing. "Is there anything else you need before I leave?"

Shaking her head, a slow smile curved Carly's mouth. "I'm pretty sure I have everything. Have a good time, and don't let Aunt Willow get out of control. On second thought, maybe you should let her." Carly's eyes sparked with amusement.

Boone chuckled. "Are you telling me she doesn't get out much?"

"Much? She never gets out, at least not that I know of. Oh, except for last weekend, she did have some kind of date. She won't give up any details, but I think she had a good time."

Boone's gut twisted. If he had his way, it would be the last *good time* Willow had with Bobby Baker.

Wicked Waters was packed, laughter and loud conversations flowing out the open door and onto the street. Kull had saved them a table, now covered with bottles of beer, wine glasses, nachos, and a huge bowl of nuts. From what Boone could see, their entire class had come out tonight to see Kell—at least those who still lived in Burnt River.

Willow sat next to Kell, nursing a glass of beer, listening to him tell a story about one of his adventures overseas. Boone's gaze narrowed on his friend. Something was up, and before Kell left town, Boone would discover what was going on. Tonight, he'd let him relax, be around people he hadn't seen in years, and enjoy his brief vacation. Standing, he walked to the bar.

"Hey there." Sarah Mae slipped her arm through Boone's, pressing her body against his. "Thanks for the good time last night." Bethany stood next to her, rolling her eyes.

Boone extricated himself, but not before he saw Willow watching them. "Steaks, beer. Easy enough." Taking a step away, he sucked down half his beer.

"I could come over later tonight, if you want."

Boone shook his head at Sarah Mae, ready to tell her no when Bethany grabbed her cousin's arm. "Come on. You promised to introduce me to your friends."

Mouthing a *thank you* to Bethany, Boone relaxed. He didn't know where Sarah Mae's sudden interest came from, other than the fact he now had a son. For some reason, single women were attracted to single fathers. He had no idea why, but it seemed to be a universal phenomenon.

"Sarah Mae, huh?"

Boone startled. He hadn't seen Willow stand up or walk toward him. "I don't know what's going on with her. I can't remember the last time I saw her, but it's been years." He tilted the bottle again, swallowing more of his beer.

"The single dad thing."

He almost choked on the beer, laughter bubbling up inside him. "What?"

"Oh, come on. Don't tell me you don't have women following you and Ty when you go the park, or store, or school events. It's like some kind of rule."

Turning toward her, he grinned. "A rule, huh?"

Resting her back against the bar, Willow nodded. "Yeah. Single woman sees single father, she's required to hit on him. It's a fact of life."

"You don't seem to have any problem not hitting on this single father." He watched her reaction, seeing her eyes widen slightly.

"That's different. This single woman has experience with said single father and knows he has no interest."

Setting down the bottle, Boone stepped in front of her, slipping an arm around her waist. "And what if this single father does have an interest?"

He saw her smile falter, heard her breath catch as he tightened his hold. "Boone..."

"You two ready to head over to Doc's? I'm starving." Kell came up behind Boone, unaware of the tension between the two.

Clearing her throat, Willow nodded. "So am I." She rested her hands on Boone's shoulders, pushing until he dropped his arm.

"Let's walk to Doc's. I don't think Kull will mind if we leave the trucks here." Finishing his beer, Kell set his empty bottle on the bar.

Neither Boone nor Willow moved as Kell walked away. Sensing she was about to bolt, Boone settled a hand on her shoulder, his expression serious.

"I know you're thinking of taking off, but don't. Have dinner with us."

Licking her lips, she lifted her chin. "Do you promise to behave?"

Removing his hat, he scratched his head. "How about I promise to do my best?"

Shaking her head, Willow shoved him lightly on the shoulder as she stepped around him. "You're incorrigible."

Slipping his hat back on his head, he chuckled. "Never said I wasn't."

The weekend passed in a blur. Kell worked alongside the three Macklin brothers on Saturday, then everyone went to Thorn's for a barbeque. Sunday morning, Kell slept late, while Boone and Tyler attended church. To Boone's immense disappointment, Willow didn't appear, her parents saying something about her need to catch up on paperwork and chores around the house.

When they returned home, Tyler almost stumbled over Kell's duffle bag, packed and ready by the front door.

"Head upstairs and change, Ty. And be sure to hang up your clothes." Boone figured if the shirt made it into the closet, it was a win. Hearing Kell's voice, he walked into the kitchen as his friend hung up the phone.

"What's up?"

Kell's face twisted into a grimace. "I got a call ordering me to fly back tonight."

Pulling out a chair, Boone sat down. Kell didn't often show any negative emotions about his work in the army, so his unenthusiastic comment got Boone's attention.

"Are you going to tell me what's going on before you leave?"

Kell's usual ironclad control slipped enough for Boone to know he'd hit a nerve. "You know I can't talk about my missions."

"That's not what I mean. Something's going on inside you, Kell." Boone pointed to his own head to emphasize his meaning. "I've known you long enough to catch when something's off. Talk to me."

Leaning forward, Kell rested his elbows on the table, scrubbing his face with both hands. Mumbling a curse, he sat back, crossing his arms.

"The last mission didn't go so well. We lost a lot of men on our team." He shifted his gaze out the window, his face expressionless. "A good friend died in my arms. There was nothing I could do to help him."

Boone swore under his breath, but didn't interrupt.

"They got us out of there the next morning, put us through routine physicals and psych evaluations, then told us to go home. Before I left, my commanding officer pulled me aside." Kell shook his head and grimaced. "I don't know if he spoke to the others, but he told me I might not be approved for more combat...at least for a while. Apparently, my psych evaluation didn't go so well."

Boone's brows furrowed. "That's bull. Everyone knows you're rock solid."

"That's pretty much what my CO said. The trouble is he can't overrule the doctors. Anyway, the team's heading back out. All except me. While they're gone, I'm scheduled to go through a series of tests and..." His voice trailed off before he slapped his hand on the table. "Dammit, Boone. This is my life. What if they pull me? Tell me I'm on desk duty for the rest of my time? Hell, I'd go crazy."

Leaning forward, Boone rested his arms on the table, rubbing his hands together. "Medical discharge?"

Kell nodded. "It's a possibility."

"How long before you know your options?"

"One, two weeks maximum. They're quick on this stuff, especially when you're assigned to the type of team I'm a part of. Missing too much can mean losing your edge." Pinching the bridge of his nose, he blew out a breath. "Who am I kidding? They believe I've already lost it. That's what this is about."

Boone cocked his head. "What do you mean?"

"They're going to decide the best way to move me out. I've done my job and now it's time for someone else to take my place. Someone without all the junk clamoring around in his head."

"What about a training assignment?"

"Doubt I'd have enough time." Standing, Kell grabbed a cup, filling it with coffee. "They have older men with a lot more experience ready to take those assignments. I've thought about it a lot the last week. It's going to come down to a medical discharge or a desk."

"Is that your head or gut talking?"

Snickering, Kell shook his head. "Both. I've seen enough of this type of thing to know how it's going to play out." Taking a sip, he sat back down, looking as beaten down as Boone had ever seen him. "I don't know what I'll do without my team. They're family, you know?"

Boone did know. Without his brothers and their wives, the support they offered, he'd be moving through each day without guidance, making one mistake after another. They were his rock, and he'd be lost without them.

"Yeah, I know. When do you fly out?"

"Six hours. I leave out of Missoula."

"Ty and I will drive you."

"No need. There's a shuttle—"

"Don't even think about it. We'll leave early enough so you aren't stuffing yourself with some worthless airport food before you fly out. I know a great place close to the airport. It'll give us time to talk about options."

One of Kell's brows lifted. "Options?"

"You know, what you'll do back here in Burnt River if you end up leaving the army. By the time you get on that plane, you'll have a plan. I'm telling you from experience, you're going to want one."

Rubbing his forehead, Kell glanced up. "Thanks, Boone."

"Hey, you're like family. I'm as close to you as I am to Thorn or Del."

Kell's eyes widened, a slow grin spreading across his face. "As long as I don't have to drink from the same well as the Macklins."

Boone stared at him, his mouth twisting in confusion. "What does that mean?"

"The last time I saw you boys, no one had a thought about love or marriage. All of that has changed. Thorn and Del are head cases over their wives. And from what I've seen and heard, you're not far behind them with Willow. Me? I'm a confirmed bachelor. If I do come back, and that's a big if because I'm going to fight to stay with the team, it'll be with my eyes on a carefree single life. Do you get me?"

Chuckling, Boone nodded. "Hey, whatever you want, Kell."

"Good. I've got a few more calls to make before we leave."

Boone watched him walk out, biting his tongue so he wouldn't laugh. Kell was headstrong and smart. He also didn't have a clue when it came to love and women. When both sank their claws into you, no man had a chance. Not even a tough one like Kell.

Chapter Eight

Willow threw off the covers as the early morning sun seeped through her bedroom blinds. Grabbing clean clothes, she walked into the bathroom, rushed through a shower, then dressed in her standard attire of jeans and a Robinson's Tack and Feed shirt. The store opened at seven. She had less than an hour to take care of her horse and eat breakfast before the first customers arrived. Most Mondays, she drove in to see at least one of the locals sitting in a truck, waiting.

She'd taken her horse on a long ride Sunday, traveling for miles in the backcountry. If her parents had known, they'd have given her all kinds of grief about going alone. It was the reason she never told them.

Willow agreed riding solo wasn't the smartest decision. If anything happened, it would be hard to get help on the trails she rode. Her phone had service over most of her property, but sporadic coverage on her preferred route—the one she and Boone used to ride during their brief time as a couple.

After spending hours with Boone on Friday, then working all day Saturday, Willow needed time to herself to process his renewed attention. He'd been out of her life for a long time. Now he seemed to be everywhere.

Pulling into the lot, her heart stopped, recognizing the truck parked right by the front door. Boone sat inside, Ty next to him, talking with his hands.

Picking up the lunch she'd packed, Willow got out, walking straight to Boone's truck, getting his attention when she tapped on the window.

He jumped out of the truck, leaving the door open. "Hey."

"I'm surprised to see you here this early. Did you place an order I don't know about?" She took a step away, giving her some distance.

"Nope." Crossing his arms, Boone leaned against the truck. "I found out last night Ty has a project due today."

"They have projects at his age?"

"Apparently. He's in first grade. You'd be surprised at what the kids are assigned." Looking into the truck, he motioned for Tyler to get out. "He's supposed to share a pet. We don't have a dog, the barn cats aren't used to people, and I didn't have time to load his horse. I'm hoping you still have some baby chicks."

"Let's get inside. I'll show you the turkey chicks."

"A turkey chick, Daddy." Tyler jumped up and down as they walked to the front door.

Unlocking it, Willow stepped inside, turning on lights as she walked down the first aisle. "Here we are. I have heritage and broad breasted poults." She pointed to two metal troughs, each layered with straw, a heat lamp shining down. Inside were over a dozen baby turkeys.

Boone looked down at Tyler. "Guess we'll take two."

Leaning over the tub, Tyler pointed to the ones he wanted from the heritage container.

"Let me get a brooder to keep the poults in." Willow glanced at Boone. "If you have something at home, you can bring it back after you leave the school."

"Come on, Ty. Let's go with Willow."

"Can't I stay here and watch?" Tyler's lower lip protruded. Even though Boone knew he was being played, he nodded.

"As long as you stay right there and don't go anywhere else."

"I promise."

Boone didn't know why he hesitated to leave. He'd be able to see anyone walking in the front door or through the back. Drawing in a breath, he shook his head. He was becoming the overprotective parent he'd seen in grocery stores, swearing he'd never be that way with his own kids. Boone hated it when he was wrong.

He found Willow standing at the counter, a brooder for the chicks in front of her, along with a bag of starter feed, pine shavings for bedding, waterer, feeder, and heat lamp with clamp.

"That much stuff for two baby turkeys?" Boone reached into his pocket, pulling out his wallet.

Willow shook her head. "I'll put it on the ranch tab. And yes, they'll need this much until they're ready to be set loose in the yard."

"When will that be?" Boone glanced over his shoulder, seeing Tyler still mesmerized by the chicks.

"At least five weeks. You might want to consider a good-sized enclosure for them. The ones Ty picked can fly. They don't go far, but can get on the branches and not want to come down."

Boone shook his head. "A horse is easier," he grumbled.

She chuckled. "In some ways. Didn't your family raise chickens?"

"Yeah, but they were my mother's thing. She did all the work. All we did was gather eggs each morning, and I didn't look forward to it."

She cocked her head to the side. "Is that why you sold them off? Because you hated collecting the eggs?"

"Not really. With the cattle and horses, I didn't have time for them. With Thorn and Del married, having the eggs would be nice."

"And you'd still be the one taking care of the hens and rooster."

She remembered how hard he worked, from well before sunup to well past sundown every day. He often made it through a day on only four or five hours' sleep. Instead of partying, he now devoted any free time to Tyler, and from what she'd seen, Boone made a wonderful dad.

The pain piercing her heart came unbidden and without warning. Feeling a hand cover hers, she looked up.

"Hey. Are you all right?" Boone's brows drew together, his eyes focused on hers.

Willow thought she was, had spent years coming to terms with the loss. She'd known of the pregnancy only a few hours before the accident happened. Still, she'd felt the loss as if it had been much longer.

Clearing her throat, she nodded. "Yes, I'm fine." Looking down, she saw he hadn't removed his hand. It felt warm, safe, and all too familiar. Pulling free, she reminded herself it had never been real, a brief fling with a boy who'd grown into a wonderful man. A man who'd never be able to return her feelings. "Guess it's time to get everything in the truck. Wouldn't want Ty to be late for school."

"Have dinner with me tonight." The words came out without conscious effort, surprising Boone as much as Willow.

She bit her lower lip, shaking her head. "I can't."

"Can't or won't?"

Her heart raced at the thought of spending time with Boone, then crashed when she remembered his words when he learned of the pregnancy. She couldn't let herself go through it again—loving him with everything she had, and getting nothing in return.

"I can't, Boone. It wouldn't be smart to repeat the same mistake." She looked up, her eyes glassy.

"What if it isn't a mistake, Willow? All I'm asking for is dinner, a couple hours of your time."

"We've said all we need to say about that night. I can't keep rehashing it. It's just too hard." A relieved breath escaped at the sound of the bell over the front door.

Holding out the brooder, she made her way around the counter. "Go ahead and take the poults you want. I need to see to this customer."

Grabbing her arm as she walked past, he shook his head. "I'm so sorry, Willow. If I knew then what I do now, that night wouldn't have ended the way it did."

She stared at him, her eyes clouding in confusion. "I don't understand."

Moving his hand down her arm to grip her fingers, he pulled her toward him. "Have dinner with me. Maybe I can clear it up." Reaching up, he swiped a strand of hair from her face. "I'll grab burgers and drinks from Evie's. We can drive out to the lake where it's quiet."

"And alone," she whispered, wanting to say no, hope pulling her to say yes.

"If it makes you uncomfortable, we can go to the park. There are always people hanging around there." He looked over at Tyler, seeing the customer walk up to him. "I just want some time with you, Willow. Just some time."

Closing her eyes, she couldn't help feeling she'd be charging right back into another mistake with Boone. He clearly wanted more than time with her. They'd always had a physical connection, a spark she'd felt with no other man. Even though she'd fallen in love with him, he'd never been able to take the next step. Not even when she'd announced the pregnancy. It was a risk to believe anything had changed. Still...

"Burgers and chocolate malts?"

He nodded, hope building. "And fries."

"You're buying?" A corner of her mouth quirked upward.

"I am," he chuckled.

Letting out a breath, she shook her head. "I still don't think this is a good idea, but who can pass up free food? I'll meet you at the park at seven."

Before he could think through his action, he leaned over, placing an impulsive kiss on her cheek. "Thank you. I'll see you tonight."

"Drop Ty off on your way to town. I'll have dinner ready when he gets here."

"You're sure, Amy? I know this is short notice and I don't want to impose on you and Del."

"Having Ty here is never an imposition, Boone."

Holding the phone to his ear, he stood in the corner of the classroom with a few other parents, waiting for Tyler to share his baby turkeys. "Thanks. We'll be there a little after six."

"You're welcome to eat with us, too."

He knew Amy was digging, which he didn't mind. "I'm having dinner with Willow."

"Oh." Her voice rose an octave at the mention of her friend. "Well then. Do you want us to keep Ty overnight?"

He wished. "Thanks, but no. We're just having burgers from Evie's."

"Please don't tell me you're going to eat there. You know Evie won't leave you two alone."

"Yeah, I figured as much. We're going to the park. I could take Ty, but…" He winced when one of the parents turned toward him, a finger over her mouth.

Amy's voice grew serious. "Not a chance, Boone. I want to see my nephew."

"I'd better get going. See you this evening." Sliding the phone into a pocket, he saw Tyler stand, picking up the carrier holding the chicks. Setting them on the teacher's desk, he began to talk.

Boone listened, pride flowing through him as Tyler explained about baby turkeys. He'd remembered everything Willow told him, adding his own spin about where they'd be living on the ranch. He ended by telling the class he had to find a way to keep the barn cats away from them, causing the adults to laugh.

When Tyler finished, Boone gave him a hug, picked up the container, and headed home, his mind swirling with thoughts of Willow. He'd been sure she would turn him down, making some excuse about needing to get home. Boone didn't let her first reaction stop him from pushing. Thorn and Del had told him if she was who he wanted, he couldn't let himself give up. They hadn't with

Grace and Amy, and he sure as heck didn't want to be the brother who lost the woman he wanted.

The one catch came when Kell asked him a question he hadn't thought through. A few minutes before dropping him at the airport, he'd asked Boone how much he loved her, if he intended to marry her. Boone had to admit he hadn't thought that far ahead.

He'd spent the drive home and most of the night figuring out where he wanted their relationship to go if he were fortunate enough to win Willow back. Boone knew he loved her—had no doubt about that. His concern didn't lie there. He had baggage in the form of Tyler. Willow had never hidden her desire to marry and have children. What would she think of stepping into the role of being a mother to a child who wasn't hers?

Parking next to the barn, he turned off the engine, not moving from behind the wheel. Jenny had asked him the same, worried Boone would resent taking Tyler after a while, the way a young boy would change his life. He'd done as she asked—taken a few weeks before making his decision.

Right now, Boone had full authority to raise Tyler the way he saw fit. He didn't need to compromise with another adult. He and Tyler had a routine, one Boone wasn't interested in changing. No matter how much he loved Willow, there'd be compromises and changes. Could he share decisions with her? Would Willow even have an interest in taking on a ready-made family?

Getting out of the truck, he put the baby turkeys and their supplies in the barn, pushing questions about Willow out of his mind. He had more than a full day of chores to do before picking up Tyler. Afterward, he'd still have to finish his work, shower, and drop Tyler off at Del's before calling in the food order.

His only worry now was how to get out of Evie's without her grilling him about his larger than normal order.

Willow looked in the mirror, feeling a hint of unease as she stared at herself. She'd broken down, asking her longtime assistant manager to close for her, then rushed home. Standing under the shower longer than normal, she let the hot water sluice down her back, relaxing muscles tense from thinking about tonight.

Changing twice, she still wasn't certain of the outfit. Figuring a dress would be too formal, she'd tried on a loose pair of slacks and a blouse. They didn't feel right. Next, she slipped into a new pair of jeans and white top. Trying once more, she forced herself into a pair of black, slender jeans. She hadn't worn them in months, forgetting how well they fit—once she got used to the tight fit. Rifling through the closet, she pulled out a silk blue blouse she'd bought months before because it matched her eyes.

Tugging on black boots, she stood in front of the mirror again, nodding in approval. Slipping on a Swiss blue topaz necklace and matching earrings, she wiped damp hands down her jeans, forcing herself to relax. They were meeting at the park for burgers and malts, the same as they'd done back in high school. Then, they'd been part of a group, her watching as he dated one of her friends, then another, never sparing her a glance. It hurt to think about it now, maybe more than it did at seventeen.

Years had passed before he called, asking her out. The invitation stunned her. For a brief time, she wondered if he'd gone through all the eligible women in Burnt River and she was next on his list. At the time, it hadn't seemed so implausible.

Boone was twenty-four and she'd just turned twenty-three. Those months had been the most glorious of her life. They'd taken long rides, gone on picnics, fished, and hiked the local mountains. She'd changed her work schedule, giving herself Saturdays off to help Boone on the ranch.

Then she'd tested positive on the home pregnancy test. A subsequent visit to her doctor confirmed it, triggering a conversation with Boone she wished she'd never had.

Looking back, she should've foreseen the outcome before pulling up to the ranch house. He'd never introduced her as his girlfriend to Del or anyone else. Their activities included the two of them, never meeting friends for drinks or dinner. He didn't attend church with her or do anything intimating they were a couple. Because of that, she'd kept her mouth shut, waiting for Boone to make some sort of statement about their relationship before she told her friends and parents. He never did.

Her hands began to shake. Lowering herself onto the bed, she clasped them in her lap, taking a deep breath. Releasing it slowly, she wondered what she was doing going out with a man who'd broken her heart, shattering it until she doubted her ability to love anyone else. She hadn't. Boone had been it for her, and that was why she'd made the decision to see him tonight.

Her heart would always belong to him. No matter the outcome, she wanted to be around him, be a part of his and Tyler's life. Even if they ended up as just friends this time around, she'd figure out a way to live with it.

Checking the time, she ratcheted up her courage. She'd enjoy her time with Boone, and when it ended, she'd close the door on their past and move on. Perhaps closure would give her the confidence to meet someone else, fall in love again, and build a future.

Walking to her truck, she stared at the clear night, making a decision. She'd enjoy her time with Boone, get to know Tyler, and refuse to become attached. When it all ended in a few weeks or months, as it certainly would, she'd walk away whole.

Chapter Nine

"Two cheeseburgers, two fries, and two chocolate malts." Evie looked up at Boone, a brow lifting as she looked around him. "I don't see Ty with you, which means either you're mighty hungry or you're planning to share. So spill. Which is it?"

Boone smiled, handing her money and picking up the bags. "You know I have a big appetite, Evie."

Her lips twisted into a skeptical grin. "Well, just in case, I put two straws and plenty of napkins in the bag."

"I almost forgot." He reached into a pocket, pulling out a folded flyer. "Amy asked if you would post this regarding a community meeting this Saturday. It's about some missing children."

She looked it over, nodding. "Sure, Boone. I'll make it a point to be there."

"Thanks, Evie. I'll see you there." He made a quick exit, not allowing her to ask any more questions about his plans for tonight.

Pulling out his phone, Boone checked the time. Five minutes to walk to the park. He felt like a teenager as he turned the corner, grateful for the new streetlights the town erected. At first, he hadn't thought them necessary, but Del and Thorn convinced him otherwise.

At the end of the street, he saw the park, a lone figure sitting at a table near the sidewalk. His heart tripped, as did his feet an instant later. By some sort of miracle, he kept his footing without spilling their food or drinks. Looking around, he straightened his shoulders and kept walking, chastising himself for acting like a boy of sixteen. Crossing the street, he inhaled a deep breath, taking a seat next to her.

"Sorry I'm late." Setting the bags down, he allowed himself to relax, even though his heart felt as if he had run a marathon.

Willow glanced at him, not quite making eye contact. "You're not. I came early to find a table." She didn't say she came early to help herself calm down. Waiting at home any longer had been driving her crazy.

Boone looked around, his brows lifted. "Doesn't seem to be a mad rush tonight. I don't see anyone."

"True. I never come on weeknights anymore, so I had no idea what to expect." The aroma of their dinner hit her nostrils. "So, what's in the bags?"

Pulling one to him, he reached inside. "Only the best on Evie's menu. Cheeseburgers with everything, fries, and chocolate malts."

She accepted the food, sliding a straw into the malt and taking a sip. "That is so good. I don't remember when I last had one. And chocolate...my favorite."

"Yeah. I remember."

She glanced at him, confusion causing her to bite her lip, then look away. He'd remembered something so simple, yet it meant a lot to her.

"How did you get out of there without her asking you a hundred questions?" Everyone knew if you wanted to know what was going on in Burnt River, you asked Evie.

"Wasn't hard. I didn't answer her questions and let her believe the food might be for me and Ty. I don't think I fooled her, but hey, whatever she believes, it didn't come from me." Boone unwrapped his burger, taking a big bite.

The comment made her think of a few years before when he'd never wanted them to be seen in public. She'd never asked him about it, too afraid she wouldn't like the answer. At this point, she no longer cared about being hurt.

"How come we never went out with friends or had dinner with Del when we were together?" She tried to make it sound casual as she popped a fry into her mouth.

Boone's burger stopped midway to his mouth before he rested his hand on the table, then set the burger down, looking at her.

"At first, it wasn't intentional. I just wanted time with you alone, without other people interfering. After a while, when I wasn't sure about my feelings, I didn't want you to suffer if we didn't work out."

She felt her cheeks flush, anger beginning to rise, but she kept it hidden with a long pull of her malt. Setting it down, she stared at him. "Suffer? I don't understand how I could have suffered any more than I did."

Boone didn't answer right away, looking down at his food, as if it held the answers. The butterflies in his stomach felt like lead weights, pulling him down. He had so much to say, and didn't know where to begin.

Shifting, he watched as her face changed from anger and hurt to confusion. He didn't know what to say other than the truth.

"I didn't want anyone spreading rumors about us. For me, it wasn't a big deal. I worked hard and played harder. Everyone knew it, including you. The longest I'd been with anyone was a couple months, and then I only saw the woman maybe three or four times. That was never the case for you, Willow. You were much more selective than me, choosing your dates the way I'd choose a brood mare." He sucked in a breath, wondering if he made any sense. "You were a prize—beautiful, smart, with a successful business. At twenty-three, you had it all, including your choice of men."

She snorted, shaking her head. "As if. I almost never dated. You asking me out was, well...a surprise."

"You accepting was an even bigger surprise." Grabbing his drink, he took a sip, then stuffed a few fries into his mouth, collecting his thoughts.

"You're kidding. Why wouldn't I have gone out with you, Boone? I never made a secret of how I felt...how I'd felt since we were kids." As if realizing what she'd admitted, Willow looked away.

"Don't."

Willow stared down at her burger, as if it were an unwanted bug. "Don't what?"

"Don't close up on me. If we have any chance of trying again, we need to be honest about all of it. You can't hold anything back, and neither can I."

Not knowing how to respond, she picked up her burger, taking another small bite, even though her hunger had vanished. Chewing slowly, she remembered another time when they'd tried to be honest, talk of a future. At the time, she'd been convinced Boone loved her, at least a little, and wanted her with him. A few weeks later, the truth had come out in a crushing blow.

"Honesty has never worked well for me. You may not remember, but we tried it before and look where it got us." Looking at him, her mouth formed an achingly bitter smile. "Nowhere."

Reaching over, he placed a hand on hers. "It was my fault last time. I wasn't honest with you about how I felt, about my fears and confusion. Admitting it all didn't come easy for me, so I hid it away, hoping I could deal with it later." Threading his fingers through hers, he looked at their joined hands, no longer scared to admit the truth. "I never thought later would come at such a cost or take so long." Without letting go of her hand, he looked away, his expression haunted.

Willow's throat closed up as a tightness, one greater than anything she'd experienced in a long time, gripped her chest. She didn't want him to see the tears pooling in her eyes or the trembling of her lower lip.

Appearing weak or lost in the past had no place in the short-term relationship she believed was all Boone could offer her. He might talk of feeling differently, but it would take more than a few words to allow her to trust him.

Clearing her throat, she did her best to sound in control. "I don't see how now will be any different than before. You weren't able to love me then. There's no reason to think you could love me now."

"Willow..." His voice drifted off, remembering the night of the accident.

"I don't blame you, Boone. I never blamed you...not for the accident or being unable to love me. Love is either there or it isn't, and no matter how much we wish it were otherwise, it just isn't to be."

Taking her chin in his hand, he made her look at him. "I did love you, Willow. I'd loved you for a long time." Dropping his hand, he stood, pacing several feet away before turning back to see her shocked expression. Taking off his hat, he ran fingers through his hair. "It wasn't easy for me to admit my feelings for you. Hell, it still isn't. At twenty-four, the ranch was barely making a profit, Del didn't have more than a few hours a month to help, and Thorn was always overseas, never even close enough to talk to." Scrubbing a hand down his face, he walked back, slumping onto the seat. "I needed to sort it all out. As young as we were, I thought there was plenty of time to get the ranch operating the way I'd always dreamed." He looked at her, his features showing regret. "I'm sorry for the way I responded that night. You'll never know how sorry."

Wrapping her arms around her waist, Willow shivered, not yet able to form a response.

"Come here, babe." Placing his arm over her shoulders, he drew her close, placing a kiss on her forehead. "We don't have to sort this out tonight or tomorrow. All I'm asking for is a chance to make up for my mistakes, show you what our life could be, and see if there's any chance you could love me again." He felt her shudder before a sob broke from her throat, her arms moving around his waist.

Stroking a hand down Willow's hair, he rocked her, hearing the sobs slow as her body stopped trembling. He didn't know how long they sat holding each other, neither quite ready to let go. After a while, she moved away, swiping the moisture from her face.

Smiling, he tucked a strand of hair behind her ear, then bent down, placing a soft kiss on her lips. When she didn't pull away, he kissed her again, deepening it, pouring in all the pent-up desire he'd held inside him for years.

His urgent kisses, the way he held her, reminded Willow of their shared past, the joy and the pain. She wondered if he thought this would change anything, erase the mistakes she so desperately wanted to forget.

The way he held and kissed her tore at her defenses. She couldn't stop herself from drowning in the passion, the way his arms tightened around her, drawing her close, creating a searing heat. They'd never been able to get enough of each other, spending hours in shared passion. She wanted this as much as she needed her next breath. Clutching his shirt in her hands, she squirmed to get closer.

As a teenager, she'd wanted nothing more than what she felt right now, his lips devouring hers, hands rubbing heated circles on her back. The woman she'd become wanted the same, her heart begging him to never stop.

"Willow," he whispered against her lips, turning her breath into a deep moan.

A low vibration traveled to her toes, then back up to pool in her belly. Raining soft kisses along her chin and down her neck, Boone pulled away on a ragged breath, resting his forehead against hers.

"We have to stop, sweetheart." His deep, raspy voice told of the internal war he fought to keep his desire in check.

Nodding, she loosened her hold and pulled away, missing the heat and intimacy of his touch. "This was probably a bad idea."

Lifting her chin with a finger, he shook his head, a crooked grin on his face. "It was a great idea. The best I've had in a long time." Kissing her once more, Boone stood, holding out his hand.

Staring at it, Willow placed her hand in his and stood. It seemed a big step, as if taking his hand committed her to try again. She wanted to, more than she'd ever imagined. Tamping down the fear of failing a second time, she drew in a breath, walking with him to her truck. Reaching it, Boone spun her around, her back against the door, his arms enclosing her on either side.

"Tonight isn't some casual occurrence, Willow...at least not for me. What I'm asking for is another chance with you. A chance to do it right and look toward a future." He placed a finger over her lips when she began to speak. "You need to take your time and think about it before making a decision. This time, there's more to my life than when we were together before. I have Ty to think about, and we have a shared past that's still painful for both of us. If you decide you can't take the risk, tell me and I'll leave you alone and never bring it up again."

"I'm scared, Boone. I just can't go through what I did last time." She glanced away, unable to hold his gaze without showing the full extent of her feelings. "It's not all on you. We both made mistakes." Sucking in a breath, she looked back at him. "I just don't know if this time will be any different."

"It might not. We won't know unless we give it a try, and I'm willing to do it. Slow and easy, no rush. Give ourselves time to work through the past and make sure this is what we both want." Stepping away, his jaw tightened. "I'm all in this time, Willow. It's up to you to decide if you're up for trying again."

A tentative smile curved her mouth. "Slow and easy?"

He returned her smile. "As slow as you want. No pressure. I do have one request."

"Which is?"

"If we do this, neither of us sees anyone else. It's exclusive. You and me, Willow. No Deputy Bob or anyone else."

She laughed, shaking her head. "It's Deputy Bobby, and he's a real nice guy."

"So am I, and I want the chance to prove it to you." Reaching out, he took her hands in his. "Are you still coming fishing with us on Saturday?"

Willow nodded. "I'm not passing up the chance to fish. I've already got someone to take my shift, so I'm off for the entire day."

"The entire day, huh? I like the sound of that." Leaning down, he kissed her once more, then moved away. "Be at the house at six, and don't forget the food."

"I'll be there." Unlocking the truck, she slipped inside, debating about asking one last question. "Will I hear from you before Saturday?"

"Sweetheart, you're going to hear from me so much, you'll be sick of my voice by the weekend."

Doubtful, she thought, but kept it to herself. "I'll see you Saturday, Boone. Good night."

"Good night, Willow."

Waiting until she pulled away, Boone took a shaky breath, slipping his hands into his pockets. He had no idea what she'd decide about them trying again. All he knew was if he hadn't asked, he'd always wonder. Regrets had been a part of his past. He didn't want them to be a part of his future.

Chapter Ten

"I can't eat one more bite." Willow set her fork down, pushing her plate away.

"Did you catch too many fish?" Tyler stared at her, his eyes wide. "Daddy says we have to eat what we catch."

"It's okay. She caught most of the fish, which means we get to help her eat them." Boone set another plate of fried trout on the table, sitting down next to Willow. "Do you want another one, Ty?"

Nodding with enthusiasm, he held out his plate to Boone.

"I don't know how you guys can eat so much." Willow patted her stomach. "Two was plenty for me."

"Men are born to eat. Right, buddy?"

Tyler nodded at Boone, smiling around his mouthful of trout and broiled red potatoes.

Willow pushed away from the table, picking up her plate. "While you two finish, I'll start cleaning up."

They'd fished for several hours at a lake not far from the ranch. She'd caught six, while Boone and Tyler caught five between them. Plenty for three people. Then she'd watched them plow through the fried fish.

Returning home, she fixed the potatoes while Boone taught Tyler how to clean the fish. Boone hadn't mentioned what he planned next, or if he wanted her to stick around. Last night, he'd asked her to spend the day, not mentioning it again since she'd arrived at six. Drying her plate and silverware, she stared into the sink, feeling awkward and out of place.

After their time in the park, she'd been unable to fall asleep, lying in bed for hours thinking about what he'd asked. It hadn't come as a complete surprise. He'd made it obvious what he wanted, and even though Willow didn't doubt his sincerity, trusting him again wouldn't be easy. She still felt no closer to a decision today than she had last night.

Feeling hands settle on her waist, she leaned back, resting against Boone's chest.

"Do you feel like helping with the horses until we leave for the community meeting?" Glancing over his shoulder, Boone noticed Tyler focused on his food. Leaning down, he kissed her neck, feeling her body shiver. "Cold?"

"You know I'm not."

Chuckling, he kissed her again, then rested his chin on top of her head. "There's a group of horses I need to move to another pasture. I could use your help."

Riding, breathing the fresh air, might be what she needed to clear her head so she could think on a more rational basis. Boone being so close made it difficult to concentrate on anything except the way her body responded to him.

"I'd like that."

Turning her toward him, he groaned when she slipped her arms around his neck.

"I'm done." Tyler stood next to them, holding up his plate.

Dropping her arms as Boone stepped away, Willow took the plate. "I'll finish here and meet you in the barn."

"Sure," Boone answered, his voice hoarse. "Come on, Ty. We'll get all three horses saddled and be ready to go by the time Willow joins us."

Unaware of the sparks flaring between the adults, Tyler made a dash to the front door, letting it slam behind him.

Swallowing, Willow cleared her throat. "I think he's excited about going for a ride."

Boone's intense gaze fastened on her, his chocolate brown eyes darkening. "He isn't the only one." Turning, he followed Tyler to the barn.

Washing and drying the last of the dishes took less than a few minutes, yet she couldn't bring herself to leave the kitchen. Even from inside, she could hear Tyler's laughter, triggering an ache in her chest she should've been over by now.

For months after the accident, she had a difficult time being around children, watching the rapt attention of mothers and fathers focused on their sons and daughters. No matter how many times she tried to convince herself the baby couldn't have meant so much to her, it had. At two months, the pregnancy hadn't seemed quite real, but the deep sense of loss did.

Willow wouldn't allow herself to flounder in despair any longer. Reminding herself she'd always been strong, she left the house, straightening her shoulders as she followed the laughter to the barn. Still uncertain as to how she felt about risking her heart on a second chance, Willow decided to enjoy the time she had with Boone and Tyler. There'd be time to make a choice. It just wouldn't be today.

"Ty, you stay with me. Willow, will you be all right riding on the other side of the herd?"

A smirk twisted her lips. "I think I can manage, Boone."

He knew she could do better than manage. She'd pushed cattle as long as him, since they were both in grade school. Besides his brothers, his friend, Kell, and a few others, including Willow, he trusted few on any drive—cattle or horses.

Willow's gaze moved over the horses they needed to move to a pasture leased from a neighbor to the south. She counted eight, a good deal more than the two he used to have when they'd been together before. And this number didn't count the three horses he was training in a pasture close to the house.

Breeding and training horses for pleasure riders or those hoping to compete came naturally to Boone, a talent he'd honed since high school. She knew he had more requests than he could fulfill, all because of his excellent reputation.

He whistled from the other side of the group, signaling it was time to start.

She knew it wouldn't take long to move the horses to the new pasture with improved grazing. The neighbor had updated his land with a healthy mixture of grasses and hay blended for horses. He'd planted a different blend for those leasing land for their cattle. Willow had helped him research the best seed mix for the animals, then placed the large order. She and Boone had discussed doing the same for a couple pastures to the north.

As she kept the horses together, Willow watched Tyler follow every move Boone made, reining one way, then another, keeping pace. At six years old, he was already showing his talent as a cowboy.

Biting her lip, she smiled at the intense expression on Tyler's face as he mimicked his father. She could think of no better role model than Boone.

Another whistle got her attention. Reining her horse around, she spotted Boone waving at her, motioning for her to move away as they approached the gate into the pasture.

"Ty, open the gate." Boone pointed to the latch. Within minutes, all the horses were inside, most milling about, a couple separating themselves enough to check out the new pasture. After Tyler locked the gate, Boone reined to a stop next to Willow.

"He's learned so much in such a short time." She looked at him, studying Boone's intense features as he watched Tyler remount and ride over to them.

"Good job, buddy."

"Can I ride over there, Daddy?"

Boone's gaze followed where Tyler pointed to the edge of a thin creek about forty yards away. "Stay where I can see you."

Nodding, Tyler took off, nudging his horse into a comfortable lope.

"You've done a good job with him."

Resting an arm on the saddle horn, he leaned over his horse's neck, stroking the animal with his other hand. "Ty's a quick learner. He loves horses and riding." Chuckling, he watched the boy dismount, letting his horse drink from the stream.

"Does he miss his mother?"

Boone stilled for a moment, his jaw tightening before nodding. "He prays every night for God to watch over her. Other than that, he never mentions Jenny." Sitting up, he looked at Willow. "I have all her photo albums, a few letters she wrote for me to give him as he gets older. She wanted to make sure he knew how much she loved him. No matter what happens, I won't let him forget her." His voice thickened on the last.

Not for the first time, Willow wondered if Jenny had meant more to him than he wanted to admit. "I didn't know her well. We were in school together, but never hung out in the same group."

A grim smile curved his lips. "That's because you always hung out with the boys."

Lifting her chin, she glared at him. "Because boys did things I liked. Played baseball, climbed trees, went fishing. All the girls wanted to do was have sleepovers and talk."

Boone watched her, cocking his head. "Don't you feel you missed out by not having girlfriends?"

Willow thought a moment. When she spoke, her voice contained a sadness he hadn't anticipated. "I have friends, just not as many as most girls. And most of mine moved away for college."

"They didn't come back?"

She shook her head. "No. One's a nurse in Bozeman and the other works for an accounting firm in Phoenix. We get together when they come home for Christmas. About once a year, I travel to Bozeman to see Alex."

His brows scrunched together. "Alex?"

"Alexandra Scott. I'm sure you remember her. The two of you, well...used to go out. The same as most of the girls around here."

She was right. He remembered Alex and the couple months they saw each other the summer after she graduated from high school. He hadn't seen her since she left for college. Boone also remembered her being friends with Willow. At the time, he'd been too caught up in his own needs to think about how dating her friends affected her.

"I know it doesn't mean much now, but I'm sorry if I hurt you back then, Willow. It wasn't my intention."

Shrugging, she reined her horse around him. "Few people ever intend to hurt another. It just happens."

Kicking her horse, she rode to meet Tyler at the creek, needing to get away from Boone and another unpleasant memory from their past. She and Alex had remained friends only because Willow had never mentioned her feelings for Boone.

Each time she thought about agreeing to his request to try again, their past got in the way, reminding her how often he'd made it clear she wasn't who he wanted. Alex exemplified the kind of woman Boone had always sought—stunning with a ready smile, an hourglass figure. Willow, dressed in cutoff jeans and boots, loved to do the same things as the boys.

Alex wore short dresses and heels, knew how to flirt, and preferred holding hands at the movies to riding or fishing. If Alex hadn't been so sweet, with a big heart, Willow could've easily hated her. Instead, they'd become close, even during the two months of torture Willow went through as she watched Alex and Boone go off together more nights than she wanted to recall.

"What did you find?" Sliding to the ground, Willow walked toward Tyler.

"Look." He pointed across the creek to what first appeared to be a rock. Then its head turned enough for Willow to recognize it.

"It's a toad. Do you want me to catch it?"

Eager eyes met hers, his head bobbing.

"I'll show you how. Next time, you can do it." Not making a sound, Willow crossed the creek several yards from the toad, then moved slowly behind it. Kneeling, she cupped her hands, gently wrapping them around the toad and lifting. Holding it against her chest, she jumped across a narrow spot of the creek. "Do you want to hold him?"

Tyler's eyes widened. After a moment, he nodded, holding out his hands.

"You need to be gentle and don't make any sudden moves."

Boone watched from several feet away, an ache growing in his chest as he watched Willow and Tyler. He loved them both, but had handled his feelings for one much better than the other. The instant she'd mentioned Alex, their easy banter became strained.

As he thought back, he realized how many times he'd hurt Willow without ever intending to. The same as his brothers, Boone never had a problem attracting female companions. The difference was Thorn and Del had always been discreet, selective, whereas he had never cared who knew about the women he dated. Until Willow came blasting into his life a few years ago. He'd wanted to protect her, guard her reputation, not wanting her to be lumped into the group he thought of as his former lovers. There had never been anything casual or short-term about Willow and his feelings for her. Then he'd blown it all. He couldn't allow himself to believe he wouldn't be allowed another chance.

"What do you two have?" He ignored the less than welcoming expression on her face as he knelt next to Tyler, looking into his cupped hands. "A toad?"

"Willow got him for me."

He glanced at her, seeing the wary expression on her face. "Did she now?"

"Can I keep him? Please…"

Standing, Boone shook his head. "Not this time, buddy. You have two baby turkeys and your horse to take care of. We're going to let Mr. Toad get back to his own family. All right?"

Tyler's lower lip protruded as he nodded. "Okay. But can we come back again?"

"We sure can. Now, why don't you set him down and we'll head home. We have a meeting to go to tonight."

Willow grimaced, remembering how she'd agreed to drop her truck off at her parents' house and ride with Boone to the meeting. Right now, she needed space from him, not forced closeness. But she'd committed to going and knew Carly looked forward to babysitting Tyler while they were gone.

As Tyler knelt by the creek, talking to the toad before letting it go, Boone took Willow's hand, drawing her several feet away. Turning her toward him, he searched her face.

"You're still coming to the meeting with me tonight, aren't you?"

She nodded, although he saw no spark of enthusiasm in her expression. "Carly's looking forward to seeing Tyler, and I know my parents are excited to have him over."

"I don't care about how they feel about tonight. I want to know if you're still good going with me."

Drawing in a breath, she swallowed her doubts about spending time with him. She knew old fears from the past were burrowing their way into her mind, creating uncertainty about moving forward with Boone. If only she could forget the past and not allow it to control her future.

Lifting her chin, she nodded. "Yes, I'm good going with you."

Reaching out, he stroked a finger down her cheek, cupping her chin. "What happened in the past, the other people I dated, means nothing to me now. The only woman I want in my life is you, Willow, and I'll wait as long as needed to prove it to you." Bending down, he kissed her, drawing away when he heard Tyler approach.

"All done. He can go home to his family now."

Smiling at Willow, he moved away, ruffling Tyler's hair, realizing how long it had gotten. "You know, it's about time I called Ashley and got us both in for haircuts."

Scrunching up his nose, Tyler shook his head. "Do we have to?"

"Afraid so. No one will recognize you if we let it get much longer."

As Willow listened to the two of them, her tension began to slip away. She needed time to sort her feelings, decide if she could forget the past and create a life with the man she'd loved for years. Boone would give her time, and right now, she'd take as much as he'd give.

Chapter Eleven

Opening Willow's door, Boone took her hand to help her out, not releasing it as they entered the county building where the meeting would be held. Spotting Del at the front, Boone walked toward him, still not releasing her hand. It was the first public display of how he felt about her, exciting her while emphasizing his serious intentions. He'd set aside his doubts from the past and decided to make his feelings known. Willow had to decide if she could do the same.

"Del." Boone extended his hand. "Looks like you're going to have a good crowd."

Grasping Boone's hand, Del's eyes took in the way his other hand held Willow's, a slight smile curling the corners of his mouth. "Appears that way." He looked at the man next to him. "You both know Detective Rick Zoeller. He's representing the police department tonight."

Both nodded, greeting Rick.

"Who's the suit?" Boone asked, his gaze on the man behind them.

Rick motioned for the man to join them. "He's a friend of mine. This is FBI Agent Dolan Randall. Dolan, this is Boone Macklin and Willow Robinson. Boone is Del's brother."

Dolan extended his hand, an edge to the smile he gave them. "Nice to meet both of you."

Boone lifted a brow. "So the FBI is helping with what Del's going to talk about?"

Dolan glanced at Del, then Rick before answering. "Several children have disappeared within a hundred mile radius of here over the last few weeks. We'll help in any way possible to locate them."

Boone's eyes widened. "Del mentioned a couple children, but it sounds like there are more."

Dolan let out a breath. "Several more than a couple. We'll give you all the details during the meeting."

Del glanced at the clock on the wall. "Time to get started."

Boone led Willow to two empty chairs in the second row, sitting down next to Ashley and Josh Wright. Saying hello to each of them before Del called the meeting to order, Boone leaned toward Ashley. "Haircuts for Ty and me."

Ashley chuckled, reaching out to touch a strand of Boone's hair. "Only about a month later than normal. I'll call you the first of the week to set up appointments." Leaning back in her chair, she took Josh's hand, focusing her attention on the front.

Holding a microphone, Del cleared his throat. "Thank you all for coming on such short notice. For those who don't know me, I'm Sheriff Del Macklin. With me is Detective Rick Zoeller, with the Burnt River Police Department, and FBI Agent Dolan Randall. They'll be talking to you tonight, and all three of us will stay as long as needed to answer your questions. Now, let's get to the reason we're here. Twelve children have gone missing within the last few weeks, all within a hundred mile radius of Burnt River. All are considered to be kidnappings."

A hush fell over the audience as Del spoke. Over the next half hour, he, Rick, and Dolan talked about the missing children, providing a timeline of the kidnappings, a map of the locations, the age and gender of each child. When Dolan finished, he turned it back over to Del.

"As you heard, no children from our area have gone missing. All are girls between the ages of eleven and fourteen. That doesn't rule out older or younger children being taken, nor does it rule out boys."

Del saw Jerry Cooper's hand go up. A friend of Boone's, he'd known him since they were young. "Jerry?"

"Do you know anything about the kidnappers at all?"

Del shook his head. "So far, they've been careful. No one has identified a vehicle or seen the people involved."

"So you don't know if we're looking for a truck, van, or car?"

"That's right, Jerry. I wish we had more for you, but we don't."

Another hand went up. "Harpur?"

"Since there isn't much to go on, what do you want us to do?"

"Be vigilant and keep watch on the children. All of them. Don't leave them outside and alone. An adult should always be present. Call me or Rick if you see anything suspicious."

"Such as?" Harpur asked.

"Any vehicle you don't recognize and seems out of place. If you notice them more than once, perhaps driving slowly through your neighborhood, take down the license number. We're a small community and don't get a huge number of tourists."

Dolan stood up. "Also, watch for trucks or vans with company logos you don't recognize. Oftentimes, kidnappers use magnetic signs on the sides of their vehicles, changing them out to help hide their identity. Use your instincts. If you don't like what you see, jot down the license and call us."

Del looked out in the audience, seeing several more hands go up. "Shane?"

"Are you planning to organize neighborhood patrols until the kidnappings stop?"

Del shook his head. "Not yet, but we aren't ruling it out. And to be clear on this, the kidnappings aren't limited to the towns. People like Shane, Boone, and others who have ranches or live outside of town are at just as much risk. Don't think because you live off the main road whoever is doing this won't go after your children." He gave a quick, pointed stare at Boone, his meaning clear. Tyler was as much at risk as a child living on Main Street.

The meeting continued until all questions were answered. Boone held Willow's hand, not letting go as most of the people filed outside. Thorn, Grace, and Amy stayed behind, as did a few others, forming a circle around Del, Rick, and Dolan. Walking up to them, Boone clasped Thorn's shoulder.

"I'm on my way to pick up Ty. We'll see you tomorrow at church."

Thorn nodded. "We'll be there." He looked from Boone to Willow, and smiled.

Squeezing Willow's hand, he turned, feeling Thorn's gaze boring into his back. When they got to the truck, she pulled on his arm to make him stop, letting go of his hand.

"What was that about?"

Rubbing the back of his neck, Boone let out a breath. "I went about things all wrong the last time. I'm not going to make the same mistake twice."

"I don't understand."

Turning toward her, he settled his hands on her waist. "When we were together before, I did all I could to *not* let my family and friends know we were together. I'm not doing that this time, Willow."

"So that's why you've had me plastered to your side since the time we left my folks' place?"

Pulling her against him, Boone lowered his head, whispering against her lips. "Guilty." Covering her mouth with his, he groaned when she wrapped her arms around his neck. His hunger grew, feeling the intensity behind her kiss.

The sound of laughter stopped them from continuing. Raising his head, he looked into her eyes, seeing the same fierce passion he felt staring back at him. "I'd better get you back and pick up Ty." Opening the passenger door, he waited until she settled inside, then leaned toward her. "Some night, we're going to finish what we start." Dropping one more kiss onto her lips, he shut the door, whistling as he walked to his side.

After dropping Tyler off at the Sunday school room, Boone stood outside the church, waiting for Willow. Her parents and Carly had already arrived, taking seats in the row behind his family, who were holding seats for him and Willow.

Pulling out his phone, Boone checked the time, hearing the sound of a truck pulling into the parking lot. He hadn't realized he'd been holding his breath until Willow turned off the engine and stepped outside. Bounding down the steps, he met her partway, settling an arm around her shoulders, leaning down to kiss her. Pulling away, he smiled at her flushed face.

"Sorry I'm late. My alarm didn't go off. Guess I was more tired than I thought."

"Early morning fishing trips will do that to you."

Entering the church, he dropped his arm, moving his hand to Willow's elbow, guiding her to their seats as the service began. Sitting down, Boone grabbed her hand, placing it on his leg as they listened to the message.

When the sermon ended, the minister didn't leave the front of the church. Instead, he walked down the steps, looking out at the people seated in the pews.

"I know many of you attended the meeting last night. Sheriff Macklin and Detective Zoeller explained what was going on to people who live not too far away. They aren't from here, but they're hurting. From what I've heard, some of the parents are so distraught, they're unable to work. What I'm proposing is a second offering to help the families whose children have been taken. Only give if you can. But I couldn't let you all leave this morning without asking." Nodding to the ushers, they began passing the trays.

Willow reached into her purse, pulling out her wallet, stopping when Boone placed a hand on her arm.

"I can put in enough for both of us." He took the tray from the usher.

Shaking her head, she took out a few bills. "I want to help them, Boone. Think about what would happen if Ty or Carly were taken." She bit her lip, her eyes clouding. "I can't imagine what those families are going through."

Dropping money into the tray, he passed it to her. "Yeah. I've been thinking the same."

When the ushers came forward, the minister offered one more prayer before everyone left, the usual cheerful banter missing as they walked to their cars.

"Boone, wait up." Thorn jogged up beside them. "Are you still up for having us over today?"

"Sure am. After the meeting last night, it would be good to get together. Come over anytime."

Thorn slapped Boone on the back. "We'll see you in a little bit. I'll let Del and Amy know."

Willow watched him leave, feeling a little out of place. She'd been with him when he asked his brothers to come over, but he'd never extended an invitation to her.

"Well, I guess I'd better leave so you can get home." Reaching up, she kissed his cheek. "I'll see you soon."

He blinked a couple times before getting her meaning. "Whoa. Aren't you coming over?"

"You didn't actually ask me and I didn't want to assume."

Scowling, he looked down, shaking his head before stepping next to her. "You're right, and I'm sorry." Taking her hands in his, he smiled. "Willow, would you please come to my place for Sunday dinner?"

Unable to hold back a smile, she nodded. "I'd like that. But only if I can bring something."

He chuckled, squeezing her hands. "Darlin', you're going to be helping me with all of it."

By six o'clock, Boone and Willow were sitting on the porch, watching Tyler play as the last rays of the sun sank behind the western mountains. Settling an arm over her shoulders, he pulled her close. Leaning over, he kissed her cheek.

"I'm glad you were here today."

She shivered as his mouth moved down her cheek to the corner of her mouth. "You just wanted some free labor."

"There is that," he whispered, capturing her mouth, pulling her against him.

"Daddy! The lizard is back."

Groaning, Boone pulled away, letting out a ragged breath. "I'll be right there." Standing, he held out his hand. "Care to check out our resident lizard?"

Taking his hand, Willow stood, walking down the steps and into the barn. "A resident lizard, huh?"

"Yeah. Ty found him a few weeks ago. We kept him a couple days before I told Ty to let him go. For whatever reason, the lizard stuck around."

Her brows furrowed as her eyes adjusted to the growing darkness. "I've never heard of one sticking around."

Boone snorted. "Just my luck."

"Over here, Daddy."

Walking to the corner, Boone knelt beside Tyler. "Yep. It sure does look like the same lizard. What did you name him?"

"Skinny. 'Cause he's so...skinny." Tyler giggled.

Boone nodded. "Ah, now I remember."

"Remember. He always ran around his box. Why isn't he running now, Daddy?"

Boone scratched his chin. "Well now, I don't rightly know. Seems he's frozen in place."

Tyler lowered his voice. "Is he dead?"

Willow stood beside them, a hand over her mouth to hide her smile, the other hand resting on her stomach. Something about the picture they made had her heart racing, chest tightening. Tyler loved Boone so much, and she knew he felt the same about his son—a boy he didn't even know a couple years ago.

She didn't have to wonder how he'd be with his own child. Watching Boone with Tyler told Willow so much about the man he'd become.

"I, um...should get home."

Boone turned at her words, standing. "You don't have to leave yet."

"Yeah, I do. It's been a long weekend and I have to open the store tomorrow."

Nodding, he draped an arm around her shoulders. "I'll walk you out." What he wanted was for her to stay, move in with him and Tyler, and never leave. As they stopped next to the truck, he moved his arms to around her waist. "When can I see you this week?"

"Aren't you growing tired of having me around?"

He shook his head. "I'll never grow tired of having you with me. Haven't I made that clear by now?"

She looked down, her breath unsteady. "I guess you did."

Lifting her chin with his finger, he studied her face. "All I'm asking for is some of your time. You don't need to make any decisions, Willow. Just allow me to see you."

Licking her lips, her gaze met his. "Come to my place on Wednesday. I'll cook."

Smiling, he bent down to kiss her. "Do you think Carly will be able to watch Ty?"

"Oh, I think she can be persuaded. I get off early on Wednesday. How about five thirty?"

"Sounds good. I want as much time with you as I can get." This time, Boone pulled her into his arms, his kiss gentle and possessive at the same time. Too quickly, he ended the kiss, stepping away. "Thanks for this weekend. It's the best I've had in a long time."

Climbing into the truck, she smiled. "Same here."

"I'll see you Wednesday."

Driving away, she glanced in the mirror, seeing him watch her leave. She knew her invitation had come as a surprise to Boone. He'd be inside her house, a place he hadn't been to in years. They both knew the significance and what it could lead to. The thought both scared and thrilled her. Maybe it was time to take another chance with Boone Macklin.

Chapter Twelve

Willow slid the lasagna into the oven, set the timer, then dashed upstairs to change. He'd called more than once each day since Sunday night. They hadn't been long conversations, not much more than the basics, but with each call, she fell a little deeper.

Hearing the doorbell, Willow finished buttoning her blouse, then drew in a deep breath. Her stomach churned, hand gripping the railing as she walked down the stairs. Opening the door, her tentative grin grew to a bright smile when she saw what Boone had in his hand.

"Are those for me?"

He held out the roses. "No one else." He watched as she took the flowers, bringing them to her nose.

"These are wonderful, Boone. I've never been given flowers before." She drew in their aroma once more, then glanced up. "Thank you." Moving aside, she motioned for him to follow her into the kitchen.

"What smells so good?"

Reaching for a vase, she glanced over her shoulder. "Lasagna. My mom's recipe."

"Best lasagna I've ever had."

Filling the vase with water, she added the roses. "Don't get your hopes up. I'm still learning how to get it right." Opening the oven door, she checked their dinner, then turned down the heat to keep it warm.

Picking up the vase, Willow walked into the dining room, setting it in the center of the table. Before she could turn around, strong arms wrapped around her waist, pulling her back against his chest.

Trailing his lips from her ear down her neck, Boone groaned. "I've been waiting three days to touch you."

Turning her around, he lowered his head, brushing his lips over hers before crushing her to him. Boone's hands locked against the small of her back as her arms came around his neck. Exploring her soft curves, he groaned, molding her to his body.

Willow's soft moans sent heat radiating through him. Feeling her passionate response, his kisses became more urgent. He caressed her as his mouth moved along her chin, then down to the hollow of her neck. Arching her back, her lips parted on a deep sigh as he seared a path back up to recapture her mouth.

No matter how tight she held him, Willow couldn't get close enough. His warm kisses ignited a fire within her belly, demanding she give in to their shared passion. Threading her fingers through his hair, she pulled him down, unable to get enough of his drugging kisses.

Feeling his hands move beneath her blouse and up her back, she whimpered at the sensation of flesh on flesh.

"Boone, please," she moaned against his lips, knowing what she wanted, afraid to voice it out loud.

Raising his head, he gazed into her eyes, his chest squeezing at the intense passion reflected back at him. "Let me make love to you."

She swallowed, a small ripple of fear racing through her, but not strong enough to cool the aching need demanding more. "Yes," she breathed out.

Lifting her hand, he pressed his mouth to her palm. She felt her knees weaken an instant before he lifted her into his arms, fusing his mouth to hers as he took the stairs to her bedroom.

Kicking the door open, he gently placed Willow onto the bed, stretching out beside her. Brushing a stray strand of hair from her face, he kissed her once more.

"Are you sure, Willow? I can wait until you're certain."

Reaching up, her finger caressed his cheek before her thumb stroked across his lower lip. "I want you, Boone. I've always wanted you."

The sound of a phone ringing pulled them from their sated slumber. Scrubbing a hand down his face, Boone shook his head, leaning on an elbow as he looked down into her glazed eyes. When the phone kept ringing, he glanced at her bedside clock. Seven in the evening. They hadn't drifted off for long.

"I think it's mine." Leaning down to kiss her, he rolled off the bed, searching the floor for his jeans. Finding them, he reached into a pocket, pulling out his phone. Seeing the name on the display, his brows drew together. "Hey, Del."

"Are you with Willow?"

Boone glanced at the bed, her body limp and much too inviting. He smiled to himself. "I am."

"Good. You two need to get back to her parents' house right away."

The urgency in his brother's voice brought Boone fully awake. "What is it?"

"Carly and Ty are missing."

Within two minutes of hanging up with Del, they were dressed and dashing down the stairs. Running into the kitchen, Willow grabbed her purse, turned off the stove, and hurried outside. Boone was already in the truck, the engine running as she jumped inside.

Neither spoke as he took the roads as fast as possible, doing his best to avoid a wreck as he maneuvered the truck past slower moving vehicles. Throwing up gravel, he pulled into the Robinsons' driveway, right behind Del's four-wheel cruiser, as another cruiser pulled in behind them.

Jumping out, Boone grabbed Willow's hand as they hurried to the porch. Before they reached the front steps, Willow's mother rushed outside, hysterical, tears streaming down her face.

"I'm so sorry, Boone," she sobbed. "One minute, Carly and Ty were playing outside. The next, they were gone, and it's all my fault."

"Mom, it's not your fault." Willow hugged her, rubbing her back as her mother sobbed onto her shoulder.

Hearing the front door open, Boone watched as Del joined them. "What happened?" Fear filled his rough voice.

Motioning for Boone to follow him, they walked a few feet away. "From what they've told me, Carly and Ty went outside to play with her dog after dinner. They'd been gone a few minutes when Mrs. Robinson checked on them. She didn't see any cars or people, told the kids to stay close to the house, then went back inside. Not a minute later, the Robinsons heard the dog barking and tires screeching. They came outside to find the kids missing."

Boone sucked in a breath, his hands fisted at his sides. "Did they see the car?"

Del shook his head. "They didn't see anybody or anything. The dog followed for a while before coming back. Mr. Robinson ran to the street, looked both directions, but saw nothing. That's when they called me."

Boone glanced over his shoulder to see Del's deputy, Bobby Baker, stopping to speak with Willow before walking up to them. His gaze narrowed on Boone before he looked at Del.

"What do you want me to do, Sheriff?"

"Did you reach Rick Zoeller?"

"Yes, sir. He's on his way. Deputy Nolen is calling Agent Randall, Sheriff McNabb, and others to let them know about the abduction." Bobby glanced at Boone. "I'm sorry about all this."

Boone's nostrils flared, but he just nodded. "Thanks."

Bobby looked back at Del. "I also called the state police. They're putting up roadblocks, as are the local police. They'll do what they can. I just wish we had some kind of description of the vehicle, Sheriff."

Rick Zoeller stopped his car along the side of the road, walking up and down the street, looking for something, phone to his ear. Slowing his pace, he talked another minute before hanging up.

He clasped Boone on the shoulder. "We'll find Ty and Carly."

Boone swallowed the pain rolling through him. It took all his self-control to not jump into his truck and start searching. "Thanks, Rick."

Nodding at Bobby, Rick looked at Del. "Dolan Randall will be here within the hour. The police chief approved the roadblocks. There's only enough officers to cover the highway running north and south out of town. State police are covering what they can."

"What if they take a back road?" Del asked.

Rick shrugged. "I've asked for a forensics team to come out here, see if they can find anything. There are tire tracks out front. I don't know if they're from the kidnapper's vehicle, but it's worth having them checked. There's a chance of identifying the tires."

"What good would that do?" Boone asked.

"Tires are meant for different vehicles. We might be able to determine if they're driving a truck, van, or car. It would be a start." Rick turned to Del. "I also called Pierce O'Brien at the Coeur d'Alene Police Department. I told him I'd send images of Carly and Ty."

"The Robinsons have one of Carly ready for you. Amy and Grace are sending me recent ones of Ty." Del looked at Boone. "Unless you have one on your phone."

Boone nodded. "I do." He pulled out his phone, his throat constricting as he thumbed through the images of Tyler.

"Send it to this email address." Rick added his cell number to his business card, handing it to Boone. "My office will forward images of both children right away."

Looking at the card, Boone's hand shook as he attached the image to an email, then sent it. "What can I do? I can't stand around doing nothing."

Del glanced between Rick and Bobby. "Can you give Boone and me a few minutes?"

Rick nodded. "Sure. I'll talk to Willow and the Robinsons."

"I'll go with him, Sheriff. Unless there's something else you want me to do."

"Go back to the office, Bobby. I want you and Joe to start notifying everyone about Carly and Ty. There's no need to keep it quiet. If anyone volunteers to look, we'll take all the help we can get."

"Yes, sir."

Turning, Del studied Boone's face, seeing fear and another emotion he'd never associated with his younger brother. Helplessness. "We will find them."

Burying his face in his hands, Boone shook his head, mumbling a curse. Looking up, his anxious gaze met Del's. "I can't lose Ty."

"You won't."

Boone sat next to Willow on the sofa as Agent Dolan Randall spoke with her parents. Rick stood in a corner, talking on his phone, while Del worked with the state forensic team outside, checking the area for anything useful in the search.

Boone and Willow had spoken to Dolan when he first arrived. Knowing all the previous missing children were girls, Boone wondered if different people might've taken Tyler and Carly. Dolan didn't have an answer, other than to say if they got a call asking for ransom, it probably wasn't connected to the other kidnappings. He also reminded Boone whoever did this might've taken Tyler because he was there and they didn't want to leave a witness. None of his answers gave Boone any peace.

Draping his arm over Willow's shoulders, Boone tried to think of something to say that would ease her fear, and his own. So far, he'd thought of nothing.

Over three hours had passed since Carly and Ty were taken. So far, the roadblocks hadn't found any suspicious vehicles. Most were locals or from Missoula. All had identification, and the few searches performed uncovered nothing.

"Have your parents tried to notify Greg about Carly?"

Willow looked at Boone, shaking her head. "They wanted to wait."

"Hoping they'll be found?"

She nodded, swiping moisture from her cheek. "He's on an assignment overseas. The same as when Thorn was in Special Forces, Greg can't say where he's being sent. Most times, his superiors won't get a message to him until he's returned from his mission." She looked over at him, her eyes red. "There's nothing he can do anyway. Right?"

Boone knew Greg would want to know as soon as possible, the same as he or his brothers would. Pulling her close to his side, he kissed her temple.

"You may not want to hear this, but Greg needs to know, sweetheart. Carly is his daughter. No matter how hard it is on your parents, he deserves to know."

Willow watched her parents talking to Dolan, knowing they blamed themselves. No matter how many times she'd told her mother it wasn't their fault, she refused to accept it.

"They think it's their fault."

"We both know it isn't, Willow. Greg won't believe it is, either. Someone has to get word to his commanding officer. If needed, Thorn can help. He still knows a lot of people and might be able to push the message through faster."

Willow's heart broke, seeing her father's arm tighten around her mother's shoulders as she sobbed against his chest.

"You're right, Boone. Call Thorn. I want his help contacting Greg."

"It's been fifteen hours and nothing. There must be something more they can do to find Ty and Carly." Boone paced his kitchen, his voice rising with each word. "Fourteen children taken and they have nothing." He looked at Thorn and Grace, a muscle in his jaw twitching. "Nothing."

Grace and Thorn had gone straight to the ranch as soon as Del called about the kidnapping, wanting to be there in case Tyler or Carly somehow found a way to escape.

Boone had stayed at the Robinson's until five in the morning, the need to take care of the animals obliging him to return to the ranch. He knew Thorn would be glad to do it, but he needed to keep busy. The waiting threatened to drive him crazy.

Willow didn't return with him, deciding to stay with her parents. Before he left, she'd given him all the information Thorn would need to get a message to Greg. An hour ago, he had spoken with Greg's commanding officer. Willow had been right. Her brother was overseas. Under the circumstances, the commander agreed to get a message to him, although he gave no indication as to when that would be. Having been through this before, Thorn felt certain they'd hear from Greg soon.

"You know Del and Rick are doing all they can, Boone. I can't imagine what you're going through, but you need to give them time." Grace held her third cup of coffee, exhaustion showing in her eyes. Thorn reached over, covering her hand with his.

"Agent Randall has pulled in additional resources. Del and Rick said their offices are inundated with calls from locals to help. We have friends out looking, including Kull."

Boone glanced at Thorn, his jaw tightening. Kull Kacey owned Wicked Waters, the local tavern. Most times, he'd been more of a father figure to Boone, Del, and Thorn than their own father. "I thought Kull was out of town."

"He came back Monday night." Thorn checked the time. "He'll be here within an hour with a few friends of his. They all want to help."

Boone pulled out a chair and sat down. "I don't know what they can do that the feds and local law can't."

Thorn shook his head. "Me, either. But one thing I've learned is to never underestimate Kull and his buddies. Some of those guys are damn scary."

The thought of Thorn, a former Army Special Forces Sgt. First Class, being afraid of a group of men in their sixties brought a grim smile to Boone's face. The first one since getting the call about Ty and Carly.

"You're right. I'd be a fool to turn down any help from Kull."

"My dad has also offered to help." Grace's father, Wolf Jackson, owned the largest business in Burnt River, manufacturing outdoor wear and selling it worldwide.

"Tell him thanks for me." Boone rubbed the back of his neck, wishing he could sleep for a few hours, knowing it wouldn't come until Tyler was found. He had a sudden urge to speak with Willow. "I'm going to call Willow."

Standing, he walked into the living room. Pulling out his phone, he tapped her number, breathing out a tired sigh when she answered.

"Hey." Walking out onto the porch, he leaned against the railing.

"Hi, Boone." She sounded as tired as him.

"How're you holding up?"

"About as good as you. We've gotten no word on Carly and Ty. Agent Randall believes this is the same group who took the other children. Still, he's brought in a team ready to trace a ransom demand if it's not."

"So your house is crawling with feds?" Boone stared at the barn, imagining Tyler running around, laughing. The thought brought a deep ache to his heart.

"Agent Randall and three others. I finally got Mom and Dad to go to their room and try to rest. I doubt they'll be in there long."

"You need to rest, too, Willow."

"Have you, Boone?"

"No. Did you tell your folks about Thorn getting a message to Greg's commanding officer?"

"Not yet. They've enough to deal with right now. Well, I'd better go. I'll come over to your place as soon as I can."

"I'd like that. Willow..." He wanted to say he loved her, but now wasn't the time. "I'll see you soon."

Slipping the phone into his pocket, he sat down on the porch, covering his face with his hands. He'd never felt so helpless, never allowed himself to be a victim of life's challenges, and he refused to let himself be one now.

He couldn't lose faith or hope. No matter what had to be done, Tyler would be coming home.

Chapter Thirteen

Boone sat atop his horse, leaning on the saddle horn as he looked into the distance. The early morning sun beat down on him, a reminder over thirty-six hours had passed since Tyler and Carly disappeared and not a single clue had been found as to who took them or where they'd gone.

Willow had stayed with her parents, unable to leave them alone. Boone knew they still blamed themselves, and no matter what she told them, they couldn't accept it. Neither had slept and barely ate since it happened.

He missed Willow, but understood her need to stay with family. Thorn and Grace had done the same for him, refusing to leave him alone until Tyler was found. Thorn's partners, Josh and Tony, told him they didn't want to see him until his nephew was safely home.

Boone knew Del hadn't returned home, spending every minute running down leads and talking to anyone who might have seen an unfamiliar vehicle Wednesday evening. His wife, Amy, took time off work and stayed last night. As much as she hated it, she had to return to Gray Wolf Outfitters this morning, promising to return tonight.

He'd finally gotten a couple hours' sleep last night, waking before dawn. At first, Boone rubbed his eyes as usual, trying to understand the exhaustion sweeping through him. Then reality came crashing down, his stomach threatening to lose the small amount of food he'd been able to eat.

Not waiting until Thorn and Grace woke up, he saddled his horse, riding the perimeter of the ranch. It gave him a small amount of peace to check on the cattle, then ride south to confirm the horses were all right.

Watching the horses graze, his mind went back to a few days before the kidnapping when he, Willow, and Tyler had moved the herd to this pasture. Sliding to the ground, Boone walked to the creek, hoping to find the toad Tyler wanted to bring home. Boone had told him no. He now wished he could have the day back, make a different decision.

Walking up and down the creek, he shook his head, settling fisted hands on his hips as his phone rang.

"Yeah, Thorn."

"Where are you?"

"Neighbors to the south where I'm leasing the land. I needed to check on the horses. What's going on?"

"Kull is here with his buddies. They'd like to talk to you. Agent Randall also showed up. They're all waiting."

"Did the FBI...I mean, did, uh, Agent Randall...find something?" Boone's voice broke on the last.

"No, brother. He wants to fill us in on their progress."

"Okay. I'm on my way." Pocketing the phone, Boone hurried back to his horse, taking off at a gallop. He couldn't stop his gut from clenching or his heart from beating painfully in his chest as he followed the path back to the house. His first thought had been to call Willow, ask if she'd heard anything. He ignored the urge, knowing she would've already called him if she had. Maybe he simply needed to hear her voice.

Seeing the house come into view, Boone noticed Kull's truck, another one he didn't recognize, and the car he'd seen Agent Randall driving. A full house.

As he reined to a stop next to the house, Grace came out the front door and down the steps.

"Hey, Boone." She reached out, taking the reins from his hand. "Go on inside. I'll put your horse up for you."

"Has Agent Randall told you anything?"

She placed a hand on Boone's arm, shaking her head. "No. He wanted to wait for you."

Nodding, he turned, walking up the steps. Inhaling a deep breath, he pulled the door open, following the voices into the kitchen. Kull and three other men huddled around the table with Thorn and Agent Randall, who stood as soon as he entered the room.

"Mr. Macklin. I'm glad you were able to get here so quickly." Dolan held out his hand.

Grasping the agent's hand, Boone nodded, then acknowledged Kull, not waiting to be introduced to the others.

"Is there news?" He took the cup of coffee Thorn held out to him.

Dolan looked at the other men. "Maybe we should speak in private."

Boone pulled out a chair, sitting down. "You can say what you need to right here, Agent Randall."

Leaning down, Dolan picked up a bag. Reaching inside, he pulled out a plastic evidence bag containing a shoe. Boone's breath caught when Dolan held it out to him.

"Do you recognize this?"

His throat tightening, Boone nodded. "It belongs to Ty. It's part of the pair I gave him for his sixth birthday. Where did you find it?"

"A state highway patrol officer found it in the bushes about ten miles from the Robinson's house. He'd pulled over a car for speeding late yesterday afternoon. That's when he saw it."

Boone glanced at Thorn, then back at Dolan. "What does it mean?"

"I'm not sure, but whoever took Tyler and Carly pulled over for some reason. We have a team at the site now, looking for any other evidence."

Kull leaned his arms on the table, glancing at the men he'd brought with him. "We've offered to go house to house around the area, asking if anyone saw a vehicle parked on the side of the road between seven and seven thirty on Wednesday night. Oh yeah, I don't think you've met my buddies." Kull introduced them to Boone, who shook their hands.

"I appreciate any help you're willing to provide." He looked at Dolan. "As long as it's okay with Agent Randall."

"As long as they notify me of anyone who saw something. You can take down what they saw, but let them know my office will be following up with them."

Kull nodded. "Sure thing, Agent Randall."

"Did you find anything belonging to Carly?" Boone asked Dolan, still staring at the bag with Tyler's shoe.

"Not that I know of. Like I said, our team is combing the area now, looking for any other evidence. His shoe is the most we've been able to recover from any of the kidnappings. It may mean they're getting sloppy. And the fact there've been no demands for ransom lead us to believe it is the same group who took the other children."

Slapping his hands on the table, Kull stood up. "If you don't mind, Agent Randall, we're going to get started. We've a good deal of daylight left."

Reaching into his pocket, Dolan pulled out cards, handing one to each of the men. "Call me if you learn anything. Even the most flimsy detail could be helpful."

The men took the cards, nodded, then left. Kull stopped long enough to place an arm around Boone's shoulders. "We're going to find Ty and Carly. None of us will stop looking until we do."

His throat closing, all Boone could do was give his good friend a solemn nod as Kull walked away. Standing, he paced to the window. Placing his hands on either side, he leaned forward, dropping his head as he sucked in big gulps of air. The woozy feeling at seeing Tyler's tennis shoe began to ease.

Boone had never felt weak, as if he couldn't handle whatever life threw at him. Tyler's disappearance left him feeling vulnerable, helpless, and insecure. He couldn't stay around the ranch much longer, doing nothing, while waiting for someone else to find his son.

Pushing away from the window, Boone turned around. "I can't do this."

Thorn walked toward him, stopping a foot away, crossing his arms. "Can't do what?"

"Sit here, waiting, doing nothing. I need to help find Ty." He shifted his gaze to Agent Randall. "How do other fathers handle this?"

Dolan tapped his fingers on the table. "Each victim deals with this in a different way. Most of the fathers feel helpless and frustrated. They don't sleep or eat, and tend to push away their families and friends who want to help them." Dolan leveled his gaze at Boone. "You aren't alone. Your need to get out there, search for your son, is normal." Standing, Dolan picked up his empty coffee cup, setting it in the sink. "I will tell you that if the people who took Ty want to talk to his father and you're not here, it could hinder our chances of getting him back. I'll also say, off the record and as a father, I don't believe whoever took your son is going to call. This doesn't have any of the signs of a kidnapping for ransom."

Boone crossed his arms, doing his best to hide the way his body trembled and hands shook. "If you were in my place, what would you do?"

Dolan shook his head. "I don't know for sure. My instincts would be the same as yours. I'd find it hard to stay put, waiting for others to find my child."

Thorn looked between the two—his brother who feared for his son and a man experienced in locating children taken from their homes. He would rather be back in the army, facing enemy insurgents, than dealing with what was happening to his family right now.

Dolan stepped toward Boone. "Give us another day. If you still want to get involved, I'll find something for you to do."

"One more day, then I'll hold you to your word, Agent Randall. I want my son found, and I'll do whatever is needed to make it happen."

"Sheriff Macklin." Del held the phone to his ear. He'd gotten three hours' sleep in the last forty, and thanks to Evie, been able to force down a couple burgers, a few fries, and gallons of coffee.

"Del, this is Pete Peterson. It's been a while."

Del's features stilled, his hand tightening on the phone. Pete Peterson, president of the Savage Wolves Motorcycle Club and Amy's dad...his father-in-law. Whatever Pete had to say, he didn't need to hear it now.

"Look, we're pretty busy here right now—"

"I have information on Boone's son. Do you want to hear it, or should I hang up?"

Del blew out a breath. Pete had his hands in all kinds of stuff, much of it illegal. "Where are you?"

"On my bike behind your office."

Walking to the window, Del looked outside. Parked under a tall, shade tree sat Pete on a fierce-looking Harley, a man Del didn't recognize sitting on a bike beside him. "I'm on my way down."

"Not here. Meet us behind that rundown taco stand at the east end of town. If you're not there in ten minutes, we'll be gone."

Del watched Pete slip the phone into his jacket, nod to his companion, and ride out. Grabbing his hat, he stopped at the front desk.

"I'll be back in a little bit."

Bobby looked up at him, his eyes narrowed. "Where are you going, Sheriff?"

"To follow up on a lead. Shouldn't take long."

Dashing to his SUV cruiser, he slid inside, then followed the main road to the spot where Pete would meet him. He and his father-in-law might work on different sides of the law, but the man had never lied to him or Amy. As president of one of the state's most powerful biker clubs, he had ears everywhere, people he trusted who fed him information on all kinds of activities. If Pete said he knew something about Tyler, the odds were good he did.

Pulling up behind the dilapidated building, he cruised through the lot, not spotting the bikes right away. For such a ramshackle place, the taco shop did a huge business. All the locals knew about it, and many stopped by at least once a week. It was one of Amy's favorite places.

He found them behind the business's catering truck. Parking in the last open spot, Del got out and walked over to meet his father-in-law, who stayed seated on his bike.

"Pete."

"Afternoon, Sheriff." He didn't bother to introduce the man next to him, but Del didn't miss the sergeant-at-arms patch.

Del crossed his arms. "You've heard about Tyler."

"It's big news, the same as all the abductions. My club may be into some things you don't want to know about, but we draw the line at human trafficking. When I saw Tyler's name in an online article, I asked my club to find out what they could. Last night, we got lucky."

"What did you learn?"

"Well, here's the thing, Del. No one in Savage Wolves is going to come forward and testify on anything I'm going to tell you. We'll do what we can to help, but it's all between you and me. No feds, no local police...you get me?"

Del nodded. "I get you, Pete. You and me, no one else." He extended his hand, waiting as Pete looked at it a couple long moments before clasping it, then resting his hands on his thighs.

"Here's what my guys heard."

An hour later, Del turned onto a side road, made a U-turn, then pulled to a stop. Grabbing his phone, he dialed Rick Zoeller, his heart pounding as he recalled all Pete had told him.

"Detective Zoeller."

"Rick, it's Del. Do you have a few minutes?"

"As much time as you need. Hold on. Let me close my office door. Okay, what can I do for you?"

"I got a call from an anonymous source with information about Tyler."

"How reliable is this source, Del?"

"The best. I'd stake my life on what I was told. I want to run it by you before calling Randall. Fact is, it may be better coming from you...since the two of you go back a ways."

"Tell me what you have, then we'll decide."

Del leaned back in the seat, watching traffic whiz by on the main road. "A few people this person knows were in a bar outside Missoula last night. They heard a conversation between some guys at a nearby table. A couple of them began arguing about a job, how it went down. The guys with them warned them to calm down, go outside if they had something to talk about. So they did. What they didn't know was my friend's people followed, got close enough to hear a few things. Turns out these guys were arguing about several of what they called *transport jobs* and the cargo they delivered. One of them got real agitated about the risk they were taking and the amount of money they were paid. Said for that kind of risk, he'd rather move drugs and girls."

Rick blew out a low whistle. "Please tell me the guys listening followed them when they left."

"They did. Staked the place out for an hour or so, then followed them again later when they left. The men ended up in an old commercial neighborhood near Missoula. I've got an address, but we have to move fast."

Chapter Fourteen

"You're absolutely confident in your source, Sheriff?" Leaning against his car, Dolan jotted down a few more notes. He'd taken the call from Rick as he pulled away from the Macklin ranch. Within ten minutes, they'd joined up on a dirt road outside of town.

"No doubt in my mind it's what his friends saw."

Dolan cocked his head to the side. "Why would they give this information to your *friend*?"

"They knew I'd get word without them getting involved."

Nodding, Dolan read back through his notes, tapping the pen against his chin. "It'll take too much time for us to get there. This address isn't far from our office in Missoula. Give me a few minutes."

Del rubbed his chin, pacing a few feet away, then walking back to stand beside Rick. "What do you think?"

"He's trying to get a team together to go in. It may be tough with what we provided, but he's motivated to do whatever he can to find those children. Dolan can be persuasive when needed."

Nodding, Del walked away again, unable to stand still as he waited to learn the up or down vote. He wanted to call Boone, give him a heads-up, but couldn't. If it ended up a bust, he'd be getting his brother's hopes up for nothing. From what Thorn had told him over the phone earlier, Boone was barely holding on. He didn't want to cause him any more stress.

"Good news." Rick walked over to them. "We got lucky. The senior agent in charge is motivated to solve this, and having no other leads, he's willing to get a team together. They'll raid the place within the hour. We'd better hope they find something."

"I couldn't sit at the ranch any longer." Boone stood on the Robinson's porch, wrapping his arms around Willow's waist. "Besides, I needed to see you." Pulling her against him, he buried his face in her hair, inhaling a scent he'd come to associate with harmony and peace. It was what her presence had always meant to him. He didn't know how he'd survived without it the last few years.

Pulling back, he lifted her chin with a finger, studying her face. "You're exhausted. Have you gotten any sleep at all?"

Letting out a breath, she shook her head. "Probably as much as you."

"Then it isn't much." Kissing her, he stepped away, dropping down into one of the wicker chairs.

"Have you heard anything?" Willow sat down beside him, resting a hand on his thigh.

He shook his head. "No, nothing. You?"

"I would've called you if I had, but no. There's been no word on Carly or Ty." Leaning forward, she buried her face in her hands. "I can't imagine what those kids are going through, Boone. They must be so scared." Her voice cracked as a sob escaped.

"Come here, baby." He pulled her into his arms, stroking her hair as she cried. "I know how you feel. It's killing me, thinking of what those people might be doing to Ty...to Carly."

His voice sounded calm. Inside, rage roiled through him unlike anything he'd ever experienced. Any anger he'd felt before couldn't compare to the blinding fury he'd been doing his best to control since the children disappeared. He wasn't a man to sit around. He'd always been a man of action.

"Are you up for a walk?"

Willow pulled back, wiping dampness from her face. "I'd like that. Give me a minute to let Mom and Dad know."

Standing, he held out his hand, helping her up, waiting as she went back inside. Staring out toward the street, he took in the scene before him. It was the last place anyone had seen Tyler and Carly. It had been the last place Boone had seen his son the evening he'd dropped him off so he could have dinner with Willow.

He didn't regret a moment of their evening together, had ached to hold her again after so long. It had been so much better than his fantasies. Boone remembered every detail, until the phone call from Del. At that moment, his entire being fell into a black hole of confusion. Being with her was all that kept him sane.

A few minutes later, Willow stepped back outside. "I'm ready. Mom will call my phone if they hear anything."

He threaded his fingers through hers. "Del and Thorn know to call me."

"Are Thorn and Grace still staying at the house?"

"They are. Josh and Tony trailered out a bike for him to work on while there." He walked toward the road.

His mind fogged, conjuring up an image of Tyler and Carly playing with her dog, laughing, watching as a vehicle pulled up in front of the house. He pictured them stopping in their play, wondering what the people inside wanted. Boone wondered if the kids approached it, Carly asking if they needed help.

For whatever reason, his mind pictured a van, although it could've been a car or truck.

"Boone. Are you okay?" Willow faced him as his fingers tightened painfully on hers.

Blinking, his expression blank, their eyes met. "Yeah, I'm fine. Just wondering what the kids were thinking when it happened."

She cupped his chin, forcing him to look at her. "We'll have a lot of time to talk with them when they get home."

If they get home. He couldn't say it out loud, hated to consider it. "I know."

Looking up and down the road, he turned back toward the house, taking a well-used path toward the barn. As they walked, his tension began to ease, even if the fear remained.

Neither spoke as they continued on the familiar path toward the creek a hundred yards away. Glancing at Willow, Boone couldn't help himself from thinking if Tyler were with them, his world would be right. He could no longer imagine a future without either of them. Both belonged in his life.

"When this is over, Mom and Dad are thinking of moving to Arizona, or maybe Texas."

He stopped, turning toward her with a stunned expression. "Why? They've been here their entire lives."

She shook her head, as surprised as Boone at their announcement. "I'm not sure. They joke sometimes about taking off in a motorhome, traveling the country. They'd like to spend the fall and winter in a warmer climate, then come home for spring and summer. I never took them seriously until they showed me a picture of the motorhome they'd like to buy."

He looked away, showing no outward reaction. "Before she died, my mother talked about leaving. I knew she never would since my father refused to discuss it."

Willow placed a hand on his arm. She remembered his father as a hard man, using his imposing form and personality to keep his boys, and wife, in line. His sons had taken their mother's death in a plane crash hard.

When Boone, Del, and Thorn spoke of her now, it was with deep affection. They rarely spoke of their father.

Looking down at her hand, his mouth tilted into a wry smile. "It isn't uncommon for retired couples to dream of going someplace warmer. Most don't have custody of their grandchildren. What would happen with Carly?"

Dropping her hand to her side, she looked toward the creek. "I don't know. She loves being in Burnt River. It's possible they'd take her with them. Greg set it up so they share custody of Carly with him. They worked it out so he could continue his work in the army."

Continuing on the path to the water, Boone's eyes clouded. "Did Greg ever locate his wife?"

"*Ex*-wife, and no, he never found out where she went. After she served him with divorce papers, she disappeared. Her attorney refused to provide any details on where she'd gone. Believe me, Greg and Carly are better off without her."

Stopping at the water's edge, he sat, pulling her down next to him. "Have you heard from Greg?"

"Not yet. Mom and Dad know Thorn called Greg's commanding officer with the news about Carly. I explained it all to them and they understand it was the right thing to do." She ripped up a handful of wild grass, tossing it into the creek. "I've been hoping by the time he gets the word, Carly and Ty will have been found."

"Me, too." Boone stared at the running water, remembering the few times he'd taken Tyler fishing. "Ty loves to fish. When he gets home, I'm going to make it a point to get him out at least once a month."

"Can I come?"

He draped an arm over her shoulders. "Darlin', you can come with us anytime you want. And bring Carly."

Leaning into him, she rested her head on his shoulder. "She'd like that."

"So would I."

They sat, saying nothing, listening to the sound of water moving over rocks. Boone didn't know how much time passed. A few minutes, an hour maybe. His thoughts focused on Tyler...and Willow, not knowing what he'd do without either one of them. Looking straight ahead, he sucked in a shaky breath, wishing he could do more than sit around, waiting.

Feeling Willow tremble next to him, he tightened his arm around her. "Talk to me, sweetheart."

"I can't bear the thought of never seeing them again, Boone. It'll kill my parents if Carly, well...if she..." She couldn't finish, her voice breaking. After a moment, she tried again. "And Greg. He'll never forgive himself."

Shifting, he turned Willow to face him, placing his hands on her shoulders. "We can't think like that. Once your mind goes that direction, you give up, and we aren't going to give up. If it takes weeks or months, we *will* find them."

Closing her eyes, she nodded. "You're right. I'm not thinking too straight right now. Sorry."

"You've nothing to feel sorry about. We're all struggling, and it won't get any better until Ty and Carly are found. And they will be found, sweetheart."

Nodding, a grave expression crossed her face. "I suppose we should think about getting back."

Standing, he held out his hand. When Willow took it, he pulled her close, leaning down to claim her mouth with his. The kiss was slow, intense, heartbreaking in its tenderness. Groaning at her response, he sealed his mouth over hers, hungry, searching.

Moving his hands lower, he settled them on her waist, molding them together as she linked her fingers behind his neck. Desire burned through him, his body igniting at the passion in her response.

He pulled her down with him, dropping to his knees before laying her down. Stretching out beside her, his hand moved down her leg, then back up, resting on the curve of her waist. Pleasure radiated through him as she curled into the curve of his body.

"Willow..." His hand gently rubbed a circle on her stomach as his lips brushed across hers.

"Please, Boone. Take all the fear away."

Moving his lips along her chin, down her neck, then back up, he captured her mouth again, feeling a shiver run through her. Raising his head, he stared into her eyes.

"We'll take each other's fears away."

The sound of crickets stirred Boone, his eyes opening to slits. Feeling a warm body next to his, a satisfied fullness claimed him. Lifting himself onto his elbow, he looked over at her, a renewed sense of desire flashing through his body. Resisting the urge to do what he wanted, Boone drew a finger down her cheek, across her lower lip.

A soft moan escaped as her eyes opened. Drawing in a breath, she reached up, cupping his cheek as his gaze raked over her. For a little while, they'd been able to put the last few days behind them and focus on each other. Reality came crashing down on both of them.

"I don't want to leave here."

Leaning down, he kissed her lips. "I feel the same, sweetheart, but we've been gone a couple hours. If we stay away much longer, your parents will start looking for us."

A solemn expression crossed her face. "And we don't want to cause them more worry."

Standing, he picked up his jeans, pulling out his phone. Checking for messages, Boone let out a frustrated sigh when he saw nothing. "You'd think they'd know something by now. It's been almost forty-eight hours without any idea what happened." Slipping into his pants, he shoved the phone into a pocket, then dragged a hand down his face. "We need to get back."

Buttoning her shirt, she finished getting dressed. "You're right. We stayed away too long." She started to turn away when he grabbed her arm.

"I don't regret the time we took, Willow."

Shaking her head, she reached up, kissing him on the mouth. "We're both on the edge with worry. We needed this time."

Picking up his hat, he took her hand. "I need to call Del and Agent Randall. They must know something by now."

Walking back, they stopped at the sound of someone shouting. Looking toward the house, they saw Willow's mother waving her hands, yelling something they couldn't make out.

"Let's hurry." Keeping hold of Willow's hand, they ran toward her.

"What is it, Mom?"

She held out her phone to Boone. "It's Del."

Taking it, he glanced at Willow, his heart stuck in his throat. "It's me, Del."

"We found them, Boone. We have Ty and Carly."

Chapter Fifteen

Boone's hands trembled as he gripped the steering wheel, doing his best to stay close to the speed limit. They'd made a quick decision to take the Robinson's large SUV to Agent Randall's office in Missoula.

The older couple sat in the back seat, holding one another. Willow sat up front with him, her hands clasped in her lap, staring straight ahead. After the initial excitement, learning about Tyler and Carly being found, they'd fallen into a stunned silence. No one knew what to say, so they'd stayed quiet, each lost in their own thoughts. Reaching out, Boone settled his hand over hers.

"Another half hour and we'll be there."

She nodded, glancing over at him. "You said Del hadn't seen them."

"He was driving to Missoula with Rick Zoeller when he called. The FBI was still processing the children they found in the raid, calling parents as they identified each one. Agent Randall was able to fast-track Ty and Carly. That's why we were notified so quickly."

"They were gone less than three days. Maybe..." She looked out the window, her voice trailing off.

"Maybe what, sweetheart?"

Doing her best to ignore the cold knot of fear in her stomach, she swallowed. "I've been reading some articles about children who've been abducted and returned. Most have a hard time adjusting. They aren't able to talk about it. Some don't speak for weeks or months." She glanced over at him, her eyes filled with concern. "Months, Boone."

Keeping his eyes on the winding road, his chest rose and fell as he processed what she'd said. He'd done the same, searching the web for anything he could find about exploited children and the aftereffects of the trauma. No matter how informative, it hadn't been good reading.

"Let's not get ahead of ourselves, sweetheart. We'll get the kids back, take them home, and go from there."

She blew out a slow breath, doing her best to calm her racing heart. "I know you're right. I'm just nervous." Looking over her shoulder, she smiled at her parents. They'd said little since learning of the rescue.

"We're all nervous, Willow. I've had Ty less than a year and have no idea what to say or do." He wiped a damp hand down his pants, his jaw tightening. "I can't help but feel I've let Jenny down."

Her eyes widened at the confession, brows creasing. "Boone, none of this is your fault. It's no one's fault except the monsters who took them. Good people's lives have changed forever because of the abominable actions of criminals. I won't let you blame yourself any more than I'll let my parents blame themselves." Her nostrils flared, indignation rising with each word. "I didn't know Jenny well, but I believe she wouldn't blame you, either. We've all been through hell the last few days, and I'm pretty certain it hasn't ended yet. The only way we'll make it through this is to go forward and not look back. We do what's needed for Carly and Ty, making sure they understand it isn't their fault, either." She stared at her lap, her chest heaving.

His face softened, jaw loosening. "That's the most I've heard from you at one time in, well...I can't remember when."

Biting her lip, she glanced at him, a soft chuckle escaping. "I talk a lot when I'm nervous."

He nodded. "Good to know."

Reaching over once more, he grabbed her hand, placing it on his thigh. Smiling at her outburst, Boone decided he liked it when her fiery passion took over. It had been a long time since he'd seen it in action.

Willow looked at her phone, then pointed up ahead. "Turn left at the light, then right into the first parking lot."

A minute later, Boone turned off the engine, glancing at Willow, then turned to look behind him at the Robinsons. "Are you ready?"

Mr. Robinson nodded, clasping his wife's hand. "More than ready, Boone. Let's go get our children."

Willow drove the car home, her eyes still red from all the crying she'd done when Tyler and Carly were returned to them. She looked in the rearview mirror, her heart twisting. Carly sat between her grandparents in the second seat while Tyler sat with Boone in the third seat. Both children were clinging to the adults, their faces blank, saying nothing.

Agent Randall told them there were no signs of sexual abuse or mistreatment. The children were found in relatively clean, if sparse, rooms containing beds, ceiling lights, and heating. They'd been fed on a regular basis and given extra clothes. From the way they were treated and the equipment found at the site, the agency believed the girls were being sold online in some kind of auction. The fact Carly and Tyler were held less than four days meant they had a good chance at a full recovery.

Randall gave them information on counselors and other resources the families could reach out to, suggesting they wait a few days to see how the two reacted to being back home. Before they left, he'd reminded them how lucky they were to get them back. The raid rescued seven children, which meant seven were still out there somewhere, possibly already sold and shipped off. The odds of getting them back weren't good.

At least they also arrested six of the offenders. The agent wasn't too optimistic about learning more, but hadn't lost hope.

"We're almost home." Willow checked her mirror again, seeing Carly straighten and Tyler remaining clasped to Boone's side. "Does anyone recognize the car in the driveway?"

"Not me," her mother replied before Carly jerked free from her arms at the sight of a tall man in an army uniform coming down the front steps.

"Daddy!" Carly barely waited until the SUV stopped before sliding over her grandmother, opening the door, and jumping out. "Daddy!" Running, she flew into Greg's outstretched arms, giant sobs racking her body.

By the time Willow and her parents got to them, Greg's face was streaked with tears.

His mother laid a hand on his arm. "I can't believe you're here."

Setting Carly on the ground, he kept his arm around her, keeping his daughter tucked next to him. "I'd just returned from a mission when I got the news. My commander had all the arrangements made to get me home." He glanced down at his daughter, then back at his parents. "I'm so sorry I wasn't here when it happened."

Mr. Robinson clasped him on the shoulder. "Nothing you could've done, son. They found Carly and Ty during a raid outside Missoula. We just picked them up." He lowered his voice, leaning close to Greg's ear. "Those kids are going to need a lot of help to work through this."

"I know, Dad. I've taken leave. We'll figure it out."

"That's good news, son."

Willow stood next to her brother, waiting until he turned toward her to wrap her arms around him. "I'm so glad you're here."

Boone and Tyler stood a few feet away, the boy's arms wrapped around his father's legs, his face turned away. Feeling Tyler tug at his pants, he leaned down.

"I want to go home."

"Then that's what we'll do. I need to speak with Willow before leaving. Do you want to stay here or come with me?"

"I want to go with you, Daddy."

Taking his son's hand, Boone walked to them, shaking Greg's hand. "Good to see you."

Greg nodded. "I understand Thorn made the call."

Boone nodded.

"Tell him thank you. I'll come by and say it in person as soon as I can."

"Take your time, Greg. That's what I'm going to do with Ty. The kids need our attention now. Nothing else matters."

Willow's heart stilled at Boone's words, knowing it had to be this way. She just hadn't expected to hear it in such blunt terms. Taking a step away, she walked to the SUV, grabbed her purse, then locked the car. Turning, she startled, seeing Boone right behind her, Tyler still next to him.

"I need to get Ty home. Thorn and Grace are waiting."

She nodded. "And Del said he and Amy would be there soon."

His gaze locked with hers, his features unreadable. "I don't know how long it will be before I'll be able to see you."

She tried to smile, but couldn't quite manage it. "You know where to find me." Willow didn't lean up to kiss him this time. Instead, she touched Tyler's head, then walked past them, following her family into the house.

"You haven't spoken to Willow in how long?" Del's incredulous voice had Boone turning to look at him. He'd stopped by after work to help repair broken corral fencing.

Tossing the brush he'd been using to groom the horse into a bucket, he clipped the rope onto the halter to lead the animal into the corral. Returning, he crossed his arms, leaning against the stall.

"Five days. Not that it's your business."

Taking off his gloves, Del stuffed them into his back pocket, looking at his brother as if he'd grown an extra head, but wasn't using either one.

"You haven't seen or spoken to her in almost a week?"

Shaking his head, Boone reached down to grab the bucket of tools and stomped toward a storage cabinet. "I've been busy with Ty."

Del followed him. "Look, I know Ty had a few rough days—"

"He has nightmares, Del. At least one every night." Boone ran a hand down his face. "During the day, he's fine. Eats, laughs, rides with me to check the stock. He started seeing a counselor and is back at school. The teacher says he acts the same as before the kidnapping." Drawing in a breath, he let it out. "Ty's back in his own room now. At night, I have to leave a light on, lock the windows, look under his bed, and check his closet. Then I read him a story and leave the door open when I head downstairs. Sometime around one or two in the morning, he starts to scream. It's the scariest sound I've ever heard and I'm helpless to do anything except hold him."

"And who's holding you?"

Boone raised his head, staring at Del in confusion. "Is that some kind of feminine side of you talking? You know darn well no one is holding me. I gave that right to Willow."

"Yeah, but she isn't here because you've left her out of your life, and Ty's."

"She's got Carly to think of. Willow doesn't want to deal with us, too."

"Greg packed Carly up the day after she got back and took her to the family cabin to fish. Just the two of them."

Boone's eyes widened. "I thought they'd all want to be together for a while. Have they come back?"

"From what I heard, they're expected back tomorrow. Not that you care, but Willow stopped by my office yesterday, asking if you and Ty were all right. She didn't look good, Boone. Not good at all. Amy went by her house last night to make sure she was okay. Do you want to know what Willow told her?"

Boone looked away, but nodded. "Yeah."

"She said the two of you weren't seeing each other anymore. Told Amy you'd said something about nothing else in your life mattered except Ty, and she didn't want to come between the two of you. Even if you aren't together, tell me you didn't say something so asinine."

Taking off his hat, he threaded a shaky hand through his hair, mumbling a curse. "She said we weren't together?"

Del nodded. "She told Amy it was for the best. You had Ty to think about and needed to focus all your attention on him." Taking his keys out of a pocket, he stared at Boone for a few seconds. "Do you want to know what I'm thinking?"

"I suppose you're going to tell me anyway."

"Damn straight I am. Willow is a wonderful woman. She loves you and Ty. Did you ever think that maybe she'd want to be here to help Ty get through this mess? That she'd want to be here for *you*?"

Pursing his lips, Boone shook his head.

"I didn't think so. Look, you're a good father, Boone. You could be a helluva husband if you'd get your head on straight and see who's right in front of you. Willow's always been right there for you. Now, if you don't love her—"

"You know I love her."

"Well, I guess she didn't get that particular memo." Del checked the time, walking to his truck. "I can't make it back the rest of this week, but I'll be here all day Saturday with Thorn. Grace and Amy will be bringing food for supper." He opened the truck door, looking at Boone. "You know there'll be plenty if you want to invite someone to join us."

Boone's mind whirled as he watched Del drive away. *Had I really said nothing mattered except Ty?* He couldn't remember much about anything the day Tyler and Carly were rescued, except bringing him home to be welcomed by Thorn, Grace, Amy, and Del.

He'd thought of Willow almost every minute, missed her more with each passing day, but hadn't wanted to disturb her time with Carly. Boone didn't know Carly hadn't been home.

Checking the time, he raced inside. If he hurried, there'd be enough time to take a shower, pick up Tyler from school, then buy some roses for his best girl. The same girl who thought he didn't want her. It was time for Boone to show off some of those fancy cowboy moves. This time for the woman he loved.

Willow walked around the store, putting a few items back in place as she moved down the aisles. Going in back, she flipped off all the lights, except the ones they left on at night, grabbed her purse, and locked the front door. Standing on the stoop, she looked out at the parking lot to see a lone truck—her own.

Before reconnecting with Boone, she'd never thought of it as such a lonely sight. Now that was pretty much all she thought about when she left work. Shopping alone, cooking alone, eating alone, going to bed alone.

Willow told herself it was for the best. As a single father, Boone didn't have room in his life for a relationship. Especially now, with the issues Tyler must be facing and would continue to deal with for months or years. It didn't matter how much she wanted to help and be there for both of them. When he'd talked with Greg, Boone made it clear there wasn't room in his life for anyone except his son. Willow understood. She just wished it didn't hurt so much.

Climbing into her truck, she gripped the steering wheel, trying to remember if she had any leftovers. Whatever sat inside the refrigerator would have to do. Starting the engine, she stopped at the sound of tires on gravel, letting out a sigh. *A late customer.* She couldn't just drive away without at least saying hello and asking them to come back in the morning.

Opening her door, she started to climb out, then froze. Pulling up beside her, Boone rolled down his window and leaned out.

"I need to talk to you."

Seeing Ty sitting next to him, she waved, then shook her head. "Now isn't a good time."

Opening the door, he got out, walking straight to her. "It's a perfect time. The store is closed, no one is around, and my guess is you're heading home. Am I right?"

Licking her lips, she lifted her chin. "Maybe I have a date."

Resting his hands on his hips, he stared at her a moment. "Our deal was we were exclusive. No one else, Willow."

"While we were together. Given that I haven't heard a word from you in almost a week, I'm pretty certain our deal is off. Now, if you'll excuse me, I have someplace to be." She turned to get back into the truck, stopping at his low, rough voice.

"With me and Ty."

She shifted back toward him. "What?"

"If you've got someplace to be, I want it to be with me and Ty." Taking a step closer, he let his arms hang by his sides, his face full of torment. "I'm sorry, Willow. I never meant to push you away." He glanced over his shoulder at Tyler. "Hey, buddy. Can you bring me the present for Willow?"

Nodding, Tyler unbuckled his seat belt, grabbed something off the front seat, and ran around the truck. A broad smile split his face as he held his hand out to Willow. "Me and Daddy got these for you."

Willow's hand shook as she took the flowers from Tyler's hand. Clearing her throat, she nodded. "Thank you, Ty. They're, um...beautiful."

"Daddy went to three places before he found the ones he wanted. Right, Daddy?"

Boone nodded, watching her expression, seeing her features soften a little.

"Smell them. Daddy says they smell almost as good as you."

Her chest tightened as she brought them up to her face, inhaling.

"Do they?" Tyler asked.

She blinked, glancing at Boone, then down at Tyler. "Do they what?" Her voice was shaky, almost too quiet to hear.

"Smell as good as you?"

Stepping closer, Boone settled an arm around her waist, feeling her body shake. "I believe I'm the person who has to determine that, Ty." Leaning down, he smelled the roses, then shifted to a spot below her ear, inhaling. "Almost as good as Willow."

Giggling, Tyler ran back to the truck, scrambling inside.

"Come home with us. I already stopped by Doc's and picked up your favorite." He watched her face, seeing the hesitation, but also seeing desire in her eyes.

"I don't know, Boone." She glanced away, unable to hold his intense gaze.

"Then let me ask another way." Reaching into his pocket, he got down on one knee, looking up to see her jaw slacken, her eyes widen. "I love you, Willow. So much, I ache with it. No matter what you heard, I don't just need Ty. I need you." He held up the ring, seeing the moisture in her eyes, a hand covering her mouth, attempting to hold back a sob. "I bought this a couple weeks ago. If you don't like it, we can find another."

She shook her head, tears streaming down her face. "I, um...I love it," she choked out.

He took her hand, slipping it on her ring finger. "Marry me, Willow. Take away the ache." Rising, he stood before her, waiting to hear his fate.

Looking down, she touched the ring with her right hand, as if making certain it was real. Lifting her head, she locked her gaze with his. "I love you, Boone. I've loved you so long, I wouldn't be good for anyone else."

A wary smiled curved the corners of his mouth. "Is that a yes?"

Wrapping her arms around his neck, she drew him to her, whispering against his mouth. "Yes."

Epilogue

Two months later...

"Willow. Did you see me?"

"Yes, I did. You're doing great, Ty." She rested her arms on the top railing of the corral, watching him make figure eights on his horse. "He's come a long way."

Boone draped an arm over her shoulders, nuzzling her neck. "Yes, he has."

She smiled as his lips brushed across her cheek. "Are you even watching him?"

Kissing her lips, he straightened, looking into the corral. "Of course I'm watching him, Mrs. Macklin. Keep your heels down, Ty."

"I'm still not quite used to that." Looking down at her hand, she twisted the rings on her finger.

"What?"

"Being called Mrs. Macklin." It had been two weeks, and each time she saw her hand, an excited shiver ran up her spine.

Chuckling, he leaned over, stealing another kiss. "I got used to it real quick."

Hearing the sound of a truck, they looked behind them to see the Robinsons pull up. Thorn, Grace, Del, and Amy were on a ride. When they returned, the two families would have a barbecue, the first since the wedding.

Boone waved at his son. "Hey, Ty. Put up your horse and say hi to your grandparents."

Willow kissed his cheek. "I'd better help them take what they brought into the house."

"I'll help Ty and we'll be right in." Wrapping an arm around her waist, he dragged her against him, sealing his lips to hers for a kiss that left her weak. Letting go, he smiled at the effect he always had on her. Shifting her around, he nudged her forward. "Get along."

Willow knew she must look like an idiot, a goofy smile on her face, as she made her way to the car. Saying her hellos, her mother directed her to a large box in the back.

She looked at it. "What is it?"

"A present your father and I had made for you and Boone. You got married so fast, we didn't have time to pick it up before the wedding."

"Don't you remember? You already gave us a present."

"Well, this is a special present. The other was the practical gift people give to newlyweds."

"Need help with that?" Greg came walking up, Carly not three feet away. He kissed Willow's cheek, taking the box out of the car, nodding behind her. "Looks like Thorn and Del are back."

Turning, she waved at the four riders. Grace and Amy had been wonderful, helping to make the wedding happen in a short six weeks. Having it at the ranch helped, as did the friends who insisted on supplying the food, drinks, and the band.

Walking alongside her brother, she opened the front door, noticing Carly heading into the barn to see Tyler. "Did you make a decision?"

Heading into the kitchen, Greg set the box down. "I did."

"And?"

"I'm getting out. I had a long talk with my commanding officer and it's all settled."

Willow felt an unexpected peace claim her at her brother's decision to leave the army. "No regrets?"

He looked behind her, smiling when Carly and Tyler ran into the house. "Not a one."

"Let's get this party started." Thorn and Grace joined them in the kitchen, shaking Greg's hand. "Good to see you, brother. How's it going?" It was a common greeting between the two Army Special Forces soldiers.

"Real good. I just told Willow I'm getting out. Our parents bought a house south of Flagstaff, Arizona, and a motorhome for traveling. I'll be taking over the house."

"That's great news." Grace hugged him.

Within a few minutes, the house filled, everyone grabbing something to drink. Willow moved next to Boone, taking his hand.

"Mom and Dad brought us another present."

His brows furrowed. "They already gave us a present."

"Well, we gave you another," her mother said from across the room. "Go ahead and open it." She pointed to the box on the kitchen table.

Setting down their drinks, they opened the box together. Willow gasped. Reaching inside, Boone pulled the gift out, placing it on the table beside the box.

Tyler walked to the table, running a hand down the curves of the bronze statue. "It looks like Daddy, Willow, and me."

"Why, that's exactly who it is, Ty," his grandmother said.

"It's gorgeous." Willow stared at the intricate detailing of a horse and rider, a woman standing next to the horse, holding the hand of a little boy. "I've never seen anything quite so beautiful."

"We sent the artist pictures of you three and told him what we wanted," her mother replied. "We're so glad you like it."

Boone looked at her parents. "We'll place it on the mantel so everyone can see it." He looked around the room, seeing it full of his family. There was only one person missing. His best friend and brother of his heart.

The sound of the front door opening drew everyone's attention. An instant later, Kell Brooks walked into the kitchen. "I hope I'm not interrupting something." He set his duffle down, taking a deep breath.

Boone took three long strides up to him, a broad smile on his face as he pulled him into a hug. "You're never an interruption."

"Sorry I didn't make it to the wedding, Boone."

"You're here now and that's all that matters. Can you stay long?"

Kell glanced around the room, realizing he knew everyone. He was back home. "I'm here for as long as you'll have me."

Thank you for taking the time to read Boone's Surrender. If you enjoyed it, please consider telling your friends or posting a short review. Word of mouth is an author's best friend and much appreciated.

Watch for the other books in the Burnt River Contemporary Western Romance series.

Please join my reader's group to be notified of my New Releases at:
http://www.shirleendavies.com/contact-me.html

I care about quality, so if you find something in error, please contact me via email at
shirleen@shirleendavies.com

About the Author

Shirleen Davies writes romance—historical western romance, contemporary romance, and romantic suspense. She grew up in Southern California, attended Oregon State University, and has degrees from San Diego State University and the University of Maryland. Her passion is writing emotionally charged stories of flawed people who find redemption through love and acceptance. Shirleen had been on numerous bestseller lists and releases several books every year. She now lives with her husband in a beautiful town in northern Arizona.

I love to hear from my readers.

Send me an email: shirleen@shirleendavies.com
Visit my Website: www.shirleendavies.com
Sign up to be notified of New Releases:
www.shirleendavies.com
Check out all of my Books:
www.shirleendavies.com/books.html
Comment on my Blog:
www.shirleendavies.com/blog.html
Follow me on Amazon:
http://www.amazon.com/author/shirleendavies
Follow my on BookBub:
https://www.bookbub.com/authors/shirleen-davies

Other ways to connect with me:

Facebook Author Page:
http://www.facebook.com/shirleendaviesauthor
Twitter: www.twitter.com/shirleendavies
Pinterest: http://pinterest.com/shirleendavies
Instagram:
https://www.instagram.com/shirleendavies_author/
Google Plus:
https://plus.google.com/+ShirleenDaviesAuthor

Books by Shirleen Davies
Historical Western Romance Series
MacLarens of Fire Mountain

Tougher than the Rest, Book One
Faster than the Rest, Book Two
Harder than the Rest, Book Three
Stronger than the Rest, Book Four
Deadlier than the Rest, Book Five
Wilder than the Rest, Book Six

Redemption Mountain

Redemption's Edge, Book One
Wildfire Creek, Book Two
Sunrise Ridge, Book Three
Dixie Moon, Book Four
Survivor Pass, Book Five
Promise Trail, Book Six
Deep River, Book Seven
Courage Canyon, Book Eight
Forsaken Falls, Book Nine, Coming next in the series!

MacLarens of Boundary Mountain

Colin's Quest, Book One,
Brodie's Gamble, Book Two
Quinn's Honor, Book Three
Sam's Legacy, Book Four
Heather's Choice, Book Five
Nate's Destiny, Book Six, Coming next in the series!

Contemporary Romance Series

MacLarens of Fire Mountain

Second Summer, Book One
Hard Landing, Book Two
One More Day, Book Three
All Your Nights, Book Four
Always Love You, Book Five
Hearts Don't Lie, Book Six
No Getting Over You, Book Seven
'Til the Sun Comes Up, Book Eight
Foolish Heart, Book Nine
Forever Love, Book Ten, Coming next in the series!

Peregrine Bay

Reclaiming Love, Book One, A Novella
Our Kind of Love, Book Two

Burnt River

Shane's Burden, Book One by Peggy Henderson
Thorn's Journey, Book Two by Shirleen Davies
Aqua's Achilles, Book Three by Kate Cambridge
Ashley's Hope, Book Four by Amelia Adams
Harpur's Secret, Book Five by Kay P. Dawson
Mason's Rescue, Book Six by Peggy L. Henderson
Del's Choice, Book Seven by Shirleen Davies
Ivy's Search, Book Eight by Kate Cambridge
Phoebe's Fate, Book Nine by Amelia Adams
Brody's Shelter, Book Ten by Kay P. Dawson
Boone's Surrender, Book Eleven by Shirleen Davies
Watch for more books in the series!